Dakota crossed the room and impulsively brushed a kiss against Ian's cheek. "Thank you."

The words, softly uttered, hung between them as the bodyguard looked at her. She'd caught him completely off guard. Those same stirrings that had been invading and haunting him these past few days increased in magnitude, threatening to overwhelm him. He'd banked them down before, but this time they proved a little more difficult to hide away.

Impossible, actually.

The next thing happened as if it had been scripted somewhere. But not by him. He wasn't given to impulse, not unless he was on the job, reacting by instincts.

Like now.

His hand spanning so that it partially framed her cheek, Ian cupped it ever so lightly as he brought his lips down to hers. He did it even as something inside of him ordered, *Stop!*

He didn't listen....

Dear Reader,

Get ready to counter the unpredictable weather outside with a lot of reading *inside*. And at Silhouette Special Edition we're happy to start you off with *Prescription: Love* by Pamela Toth, the next in our MONTANA MAVERICKS: GOLD RUSH GROOMS continuity. When a visiting medical resident—a gorgeous California girl—winds up assigned to Thunder Canyon General Hospital, she thinks of it as a temporary detour—until she meets the town's most eligible doctor! He soon has her thinking about settling down—permanently....

Crystal Green's *A Tycoon in Texas*, the next in THE FORTUNES OF TEXAS: REUNION continuity, features a workaholic businesswoman whose concentration is suddenly shaken by her devastatingly handsome new boss. Reader favorite Marie Ferrarella begins a new miniseries, THE CAMEO— about a necklace with special romantic powers—with *Because a Husband Is Forever*, in which a talk show hostess is coerced into taking on a bodyguard. Only, she had no idea he'd take his job title literally! In *Their Baby Miracle* by Lilian Darcy, a couple who'd called it quits months ago is brought back together by the premature birth of their child. Patricia Kay's *You've Got Game*, next in her miniseries THE HATHAWAYS OF MORGAN CREEK, gives us a couple who are constantly at each other's throats in real life—but their online relationship is another story altogether. And in *Picking Up the Pieces* by Barbara Gale, a world-famous journalist and a former top model risk scandal by following their hearts instead of their heads....

Enjoy them all, and please come back next month for six sensational romances, all from Silhouette Special Edition!

All the best,

Gail Chasan
Senior Editor

Please address questions and book requests to:
Silhouette Reader Service
U.S.: 3010 Walden Ave., P.O. Box 1325, Buffalo, NY 14269
Canadian: P.O. Box 609, Fort Erie, Ont. L2A 5X3

BECAUSE A HUSBAND IS
Forever

MARIE FERRARELLA

SPECIAL EDITION®
Published by Silhouette Books
America's Publisher of Contemporary Romance

To
Nancy Neubert
and old friendships
renewed

 SILHOUETTE BOOKS

ISBN 0-373-24671-4

BECAUSE A HUSBAND IS FOREVER

Copyright © 2005 by Marie Rydzynski Ferrarella

This edition published by arrangement with Harlequin Books S.A.

Visit Silhouette Books at www.eHarlequin.com

Printed in U.S.A.

Books by Marie Ferrarella in Miniseries

MARIE FERRARELLA

This RITA® Award-winning author has written over one hundred and thirty books for Silhouette, some under the name Marie Nicole. Her romances are beloved by fans worldwide.

October 8, 1861

My dearest love,

I hope this letter finds you and that you are well and whole. That is the worst of this awful war, the not knowing where you are and if you are. I tell myself that in my heart, I would know if you are no longer among the living. That if you were taken from me in body as well as in spirit, some piece of my heart would surely wither and die because it only beats for you. Each evening I press a kiss to my fingers and touch the cameo you gave me—the very same one I shall not remove until you are standing right here beside me—and pray that in the morning I will rise and look out my window to see you coming over the ridge. It is what sustains me in these dark hours.

I miss you and love you more each day.

Your Amanda

Prologue

June 1, 1861

Amanda Deveaux looked at the cameo in her hand. Embossed on the delicate Wedgwood-blue oval was the profile of a young Greek woman, carved in ivory. It was the most beautiful thing she had ever seen, even though her vision was blurred because of the tears in her eyes.

She gazed up at the man who had given the cameo to her. Lt. William Slattery of the Confederate Army. Her Will, dashingly handsome in his new gray uniform, a uniform she had sewn for him herself. She was achingly proud of him for what he was about to do. And heartsick about it at the same time.

"I want you to wear this, Amanda." Will took the cameo from her and tied the black velvet ribbon at the back of her neck. "Promise me that you'll wear it until I can come home to make you my bride."

"But why can't I marry you now?" she pleaded.

Will glanced over at the stone-faced woman who stood several feet away, guarding her precious daughter. "Because," he told her, "a lady doesn't hurriedly get married like some penniless servant girl."

Amanda didn't care about tradition, only that the man she loved was going away for who knew how long. "I don't want to be a lady. I want to be your wife."

"You'll be both when I come back. Promise you'll wait for me," he repeated.

She clutched his hand, ignoring her mother's reproving looks. Her mother had never liked Will. His family didn't have enough money to suit her. As if money could ever be the measure of a man's worth.

"You know I will. From the first moment I saw you until the last moment I'll draw breath, there's only you, my darling," she whispered to him.

Will kissed her hand in the tradition of the times. And then, because he was young and in love and this would be the last time that they would be together, he drew her into his arms and kissed the woman he'd loved since he was a small boy.

He kissed her long and hard, fashioning a moment

and a memory that would last him through however many days and weeks and months he would have to be away. He had to fight a war he had never asked for. A war that his young honor demanded he fight. He hadn't bought his way out the way some others of his class had. They had sent in paid substitutes to fight in their places. To die in their stead if that was the way of it.

The son of a very small plantation owner, Will's honor forbade him to allow others to brave danger in his place. But, oh, his heart felt as if it was breaking as he stood there, the April wind ruffling his hair, kissing the woman he would rather have died for than leave.

"I believe it is time to take your leave, Lieutenant," Belinda Deveaux told him sharply.

He took a step back and looked at Amanda, sealing her image in his mind. "Wait for me," he begged her again.

"Forever if I have to."

Clutching the cameo to her, Amanda waved as Will mounted his horse and then rode away. She waved until the horse and rider had long disappeared from view.

Amanda ignored the disparaging sound her mother made. It faded into the background, muted by the sound of her breaking heart.

"Forever," she repeated in a fierce whisper.

Chapter One

Present Day

"It's lovely, isn't it?"

The voice, soft, unobtrusive, felt as if it had slipped into her consciousness via her mind rather than registering the regular way, by way of her ears.

Surprised, Dakota Delany glanced up from the see-through counter with its collection of estate jewelry and one-of-a-kind pieces to see a motherly woman, who watched her with eyes that were incredibly blue. And incredibly kind.

Dakota would have sworn that she was alone in the

small showroom area of the upstate New York antique store, with its creaking floorboards and not quite airtight windows. When she'd entered fifteen minutes ago, there hadn't been a salesperson to be seen. It took her a moment to process the sudden appearance of another person within the rather small area, without so much as a telltale squeak from the floorboards.

If she were being honest with herself, Dakota really didn't know what she was even doing here. She'd never had much of a penchant for antiques nor a desire to haunt the small shops along the street that hosted them. But an unshakable restlessness had put her behind the wheel of her blazing-red BMW this morning. Dawn had seen her driving away from New York City, making her way upstate, her path marked by a parade of trees whose leaves were turning all the festive colors of fall.

She didn't feel very festive.

Dakota wasn't really sure why she kept on driving or where she was going. It wasn't as if she could just allow herself to get lost for an unlimited amount of time. She had a live show to tape as of two o'clock this afternoon, the way she did every afternoon, Monday through Friday. That meant she had to return by noon or risk having her production assistant, who was, as well, her best friend, succumb to the heart attack MacKenzie Ryan always threatened her with if things weren't progressing according to schedule.

Schedule.

Hell, if things had been progressing according to

schedule, she and Dr. John Jackson would be standing side by side, maybe even here in this little, out-of-the-way antique store, picking out their wedding rings. She'd thought her relationship with John was heading down the aisle. To a wedding. To the altar. For a brief, shining moment she'd actually believed that she'd finally found a man who didn't want anything from her except her. She'd found a man with whom she could share forever, have the kind of life her parents had.

John Jackson didn't need her name or her fame, not to mention her money, to try to get ahead. The good doctor was a celebrity of sorts in his own right. He was the head of a very lucrative private practice and was currently one of the most sought-after plastic surgeons on the East Coast.

Trouble was, on occasion the good doctor also liked to throw himself into his work—after the fact. Dakota had heard the rumors, but once her mind was made up that this was the man she was going to marry, she had refused to believe them. Having been raised in the entertainment business—thanks to a newscaster father and a mother and grandfather who between them had been in almost every B-grade movie ever written—and having spent the last four years as the star of her own daytime talk show, *And Now a Word from Dakota,* she knew very well how baseless rumors could be.

Except that these rumors had turned out to be not so baseless. These rumors had turned out to be true. She'd come home early from a taping one afternoon, seeking a respite after working with a particularly difficult starlet, and wound up catching John, also home early, trying on one of his remodeled patients for size.

Her heart and confidence had been shattered in one lightning-swift blow.

Now the engagement was off, John had moved out to some Park Avenue address, and she was single again.

And hating it.

But at twenty-nine, she had also become resigned to the fact that she was probably going to remain that way for a very long time, if not forever. Men just weren't worth the trouble, she'd decided during her drive up this morning. Besides, she had a full life. Between work and the occasional visits to her family, she didn't have time to focus on the fact that there were no one else's dishes in the sink but hers, that the only clothes strewn around the apartment were hers.

"Would you like me to take the necklace out to show you?"

Even as the woman asked the question, she was removing the cameo that had caught Dakota's eye.

It was a lovely piece, but not extraordinary by any stretch of the imagination. A small profile of a woman set against a field of Wedgwood blue and threaded onto a black velvet ribbon—new by the looks of it. There was nothing unusual about the small piece of jewelry to set it apart from the rest. And yet, as she'd walked through the store, browsing but not really seeing, Dakota found her eyes inexplicably drawn to the cameo.

Still, she wasn't really here to buy anything, only to kill time. She shook her head. "No, I—"

The protest came a beat too late. The woman with the fluffy gray hair and compelling smile already had the cameo out. She held it up for Dakota's approval.

For a moment the face of the woman in the cameo was trapped in a sunbeam.

"It has a legend behind it, you know," the woman told Dakota softly.

"A legend?"

She was too much of her parents' daughter not to be drawn in by the promise of a story, a history. Dakota could feel her interest being aroused as if it was a physical thing.

The woman came around from behind the counter. Short, round, she had almost a cherubic appearance. If she were casting Mrs. Claus in a play, Dakota thought, the woman would have been perfect.

The woman's blue eyes gleamed with vibrancy as she spoke. "Yes. It's said to have once belonged to a South-ern belle, given to her by her fiancé just before he rode off to war in 1861. Her name was Amanda Deveaux. His was William Slattery, a handsome young lieutenant in the Confederate Army. William put this around her neck and made her promise to wear the cameo until he could return to marry her."

The sunbeam still held the woman in the cameo in its embrace. Dakota found she couldn't draw her eyes away from it. Though injured by love, at bottom she was still a romantic. "And did he?"

Rather than answer directly, the older woman smiled enigmatically. Taking the cameo, she stood up on her toes and gently placed it around Dakota's neck.

"Why don't you try it on?" the woman coaxed softly as she tied the two ends of the velvet together at the nape of Dakota's neck. Stepping back, she looked at Dakota and nodded her approval. "It suits you."

The delicate oval dipped into the hollow of her throat. Dakota lightly slid her fingers over the necklace, touching it. "Does it?"

The woman nodded again, a wayward breeze that had sneaked in through the open casement playing with the ends of her hair. "They say that whoever wears it will have her own one true love come into her life. And once that happens, once she knows that this is the man she is to spend eternity with, she has to pass the cameo on to someone else so that the magic can continue."

"Magic," Dakota echoed. Did anyone still believe in magic? She certainly didn't. The woman took out a small, sterling-silver-framed mirror and handed it to her. Dakota looked at herself. When she glanced back at the woman, her smile was ever-so-slightly self-deprecating. "I don't feel any magic."

The woman laughed to herself, shaking her head as if she'd just heard something very foolish uttered in innocence. "Magic doesn't come riding on a bolt of lightning, my dear," she assured Dakota gently as she stepped back behind the counter. "Real magic slips in without you noticing and unfolds its power very quietly. Before you know it, it's taken a firm root inside your soul."

Dakota sincerely had her doubts about that. She didn't believe in magic or cameos that came equipped with magical powers. But there was no denying that the cameo was truly lovely.

And she deserved a pick-me-up, she decided.

Dakota handed the mirror back to the woman. "I'll take it."

The woman eyed her knowingly. If she didn't know better, Dakota would have concluded that the woman's smile was slowly seeping into her being. "I thought you might," the woman was saying. "The moment I saw you walk into the store, I knew the cameo was meant for you."

Dakota frowned slightly, puzzled. The shop didn't look as if it was wired with a surveillance system. It looked barely able to support the wiring for the overhead lights. "I didn't see you when I came in."

The smile on the woman's face did not falter. "But I saw you."

About to ask where the woman could have hidden in the small, cluttered room in order to observe her without being noticed, Dakota heard the ancient grandfather clock in the corner begin to chime the hour.

Ten o'clock.

How was that possible? It hadn't taken that long to drive up here, had it? And yet the hours seemed to have melted into oblivion. Had she been lost in her own thoughts that long?

Her eyes met the woman's in surprise.

"You'd better start getting back, or you might miss your show," the woman told her. Taking out a pad, she began to write up the sale. Surprised, Dakota opened her mouth to say something. Second-guessing her response, the woman's smile widened another several watts. "You know, we do get all the major channels out here. Even have a computer or two around, although I don't really like the annoying little things."

The comment seemed appropriate. The area seemed so off the beaten path, Dakota would have been less surprised to have stumbled over Rip Van Winkle than to hear that the houses were wired for cable or had computers in their living rooms.

Dakota glanced at her watch. The woman was right. She had to be getting back before it was too late. She touched the cameo at her throat again, reluctant to part with her new acquisition.

"I think I'll wear it."

"Thought you might." After ringing up the sale, the woman handed her a small pouch.

Taking out her checkbook, Dakota glanced at the dark-green velvet pouch. "What's this?"

"It's for the cameo. You can place it in here when it comes time for you to give it to the next person."

Dakota tore off the check, a smile playing on her lips. "After I find true love."

The woman nodded gravely. Her faith seemed unshakable. "After."

Moving the check along the counter to the woman, Dakota shook her head. "I don't think I'll be needing the pouch."

Picking up the velvet item, the woman pressed it into Dakota's hand.

"You will," she told her with certainty.

Dakota was still thinking about the unusual little woman and her shop as she parked her car in the underground garage beneath the TV studio's building. Although her life of late had been a little bleak, Dakota found that she couldn't suppress or erase the smile that had taken possession of her lips.

Maybe she could go back sometime and have the woman—whose name she hadn't even gotten—as a guest on the show, she thought as she entered the elevator. It was lovely finding unusual and interesting people. Most of the time, she was in contact with people who were hurrying through life much too quickly to enjoy what was around them or even what they'd earned for themselves along the way.

"Physician, heal thyself," Dakota muttered under her breath as she sailed into her dressing room. Definitely the wrong metaphor, she thought. Physicians were the last group she wanted contact with. But even that slip didn't take the edge off her upbeat mood.

She fingered her cameo, as if for luck, even as she silently scoffed at herself. The only thing the cameo was going to bring her was compliments. True love existed in fairy tales and, on rare occasions, in other people's lives. People like her parents who were part of another generation. Somehow true love had gotten lost in this hurry-up world through which she and others found themselves navigating.

As she gained her dressing room, Dakota nodded at the makeup girl who was in there ahead of her. Alicia's face lit up and she went to work, although there wasn't much to do. "You've got perfect skin tones." It was the first thing the young woman had said to her when they met. "If everyone was like you, I'd be out of a job."

"Hi, Alicia, sorry I'm running late." Not bothering to sit, she presented herself to the makeup artist, her face upturned.

Alicia wasn't alone in the room. There, biting her nails in typical nervous fashion, was MacKenzie. The second Dakota entered the brightly lit room, MacKenzie sighed audibly.

"Oh, thank God you've finally shown up. Do you realize what time it is?" With one gnawed fingertip, she pointed to her wristwatch. "I was going to call out the National Guard to find you."

Dakota was accustomed to MacKenzie's dramatic moments. They'd been roommates in college in California. Dakota, the blond, statuesque native, took it upon herself to show around the petite, dark-haired transplanted Bostonian. They'd come out to New York together to take the town by storm. Thanks to a few words

Dakota's father had put in for them with the head of the studio, they pretty much had.

Dakota tilted her head toward the light as Alicia put on the final strokes. "They have more important things to do than look for me, Zee."

"In case you hadn't noticed, so do I." Without preamble, she took Dakota's purse from her and flipped open the section where her cell phone was usually housed. "So, it *is* here." To underscore her point, MacKenzie took the small silver cell out and held it up. Her tone and frown were both accusing. "The object of having a cell phone, Dakota, is so that people can call you when they're in the middle of having a heart attack."

Dakota took her cell back and tucked it into her purse before depositing the latter in the bottom drawer of the vanity table. "I wanted to be alone."

MacKenzie pressed her lips together. Her eyes searched Dakota's face, looking for a telltale sign that she was about to break. It wasn't like her just to take off like that without leaving some kind of word. "I was afraid you'd do something drastic."

Close as they were, Dakota didn't like to expose her feelings. Especially not when there was a third party present. Her voice lowered. "Over John? Please, I'm not some teenager."

They'd known each other too long for pretenses. MacKenzie had never thought she'd see her gregarious friend give her heart to any man. When it happened, she held her breath, waiting for a shoe to drop, praying it wouldn't. But it had. With a resounding thud.

"No," MacKenzie said quietly in a tone that matched Dakota's, "you're a grown woman whose heart was stomped on by a big ape in combat boots."

Dakota waved a dismissive hand at the words. "Past history."

Glancing at her makeup artist, Dakota held out her hand for the lipstick she favored. Alicia dug the tube out of her makeup caddy and placed it in Dakota's palm. Without benefit of mirror, Dakota did the honors quickly. Finished, she handed the tube back to Alicia and squared her shoulders.

She was going to wear what she had on, she decided. "Now let's move on to our present history."

But as she began to walk out of her dressing room, MacKenzie placed a hand on her shoulder, stopping her. "Small problem."

Dakota narrowed her eyes. "What kind of small problem?"

"That animal trainer who was scheduled to be on the show—"

Dakota nodded. It was Monday. She'd gone over the week's guest-star list, skimming over their biographies and trying to get to know a little about them before she faced them on her program. "Fearless Frederick. What about him?"

"Seems that Fearless was taken to the emergency room last night. One of his animals decided to challenge his title and took off the tip of one of his fingers. I hear Fearless turned the E.R. blue."

Dakota stifled a shiver, trying not to envision the gruesome sight. "Is he okay?"

"They sewed it back on, but needless to say, you won't be holding on to one of his trained snakes today."

"Can't say I'm really disappointed." Though she was game for anything, there were definitely things that went to the bottom of her list. Holding wriggling snakes and animals that viewed her as a substitute for lunch sank right down to that level.

MacKenzie resumed walking toward the set. Dakota fell into step beside her. "Fortunately, I had a backup plan."

Dakota laughed under her breath. Her best friend had always been an overachiever. Had she been on the *Titanic,* the diminutive woman would have found a way to float the ship to safety.

"Never doubted it for a second. So, who am I interviewing?"

"No!"

The deep male voice rang out with dark authority that made the stagehand in the distance jump. MacKenzie rolled her eyes. "Him."

Making a half turn, Dakota temporarily abandoned her path to the stage and instead followed the single word to its source. Nothing like meeting the guest just before the show, she thought.

She looked to her right at MacKenzie. "And 'him' being?"

MacKenzie, shorter than her boss and friend by some three inches, clutched her clipboard to her chest as she lengthened her stride and hurried to keep up. "Ian Russell. Of Russell and Taylor, bodyguards to the rich and famous," she added when Dakota looked at her quizzically.

Dakota remembered the names. They were the former homicide detectives. The two men were scheduled for the end of the week. She decided that the bodyguard business must be slow to be able to get them on such short notice.

"You come near me with that powder brush, and you're going to find yourself walking a whole lot stiffer," the man in the guest-star chair warned Albert, their head makeup artist, just as Dakota rounded the corner and came on the scene.

Highly frustrated, the makeup artist rolled his small dark eyes and looked helplessly at Dakota. "Dakota…?"

A wealth of emotions and entreaties were locked into the single intonation. Dakota rose to the occasion. Smile in place, she took the brush from Albert with one hand while placing the other on the annoyed guest's chest. Dakota gently but firmly pushed the tall, dark, brooding man back into the chair he was attempting to vacate.

Apparently caught off guard, the man gave little resistance. There was no doubt in Dakota's mind that, had her guest star resisted, she could have jumped up and down on his chest with her full body weight and made no impression whatsoever. Unless he wore armor, her hand had come in contact with rock in human form. Splaying her fingers wider, Dakota wasn't sure she even detected a heartbeat.

"Hi," she murmured, "I'm Dakota Delany, and you really don't want to come off looking like Casper the Friendly Ghost."

Staring at her, realizing introductions were necessary, he began saying, "I'm Ian Russell and—" The rest was swallowed up as Dakota began to deftly apply powder to the rugged planes and angles of a face that could have easily belonged to Hollywood's newest action star. Damn, but he was attractive. She could see women lining up six deep to avail themselves of his services. Some of which might even have had something remotely to do with bodyguard work.

As she applied the brush in short strokes that seemed to vibrate down her arm into her own soul, her eyes held his for a very long moment. The magic she'd laughingly told the woman in the antique store she was waiting for felt as if it had just arrived.

She found herself struggling, just for a single heartbeat, to remove the brush from the man's face. But for that moment she felt as if the brush was an extension of her fingers. Very odd.

"There," she finally murmured, hardly aware of forming the word. "Done."

A deep laugh from the next chair brought Dakota back to her surroundings. Tilting her head, she spared a glance at the other man in the area. Dakota assumed the brown-haired, green-eyed man to be Randy Taylor, Ian's partner.

"I'm afraid there's little chance that anyone's going to mistake Ian for a friendly anything. That scowl was chiseled in when he was three days old. Been there ever since," Randy said, grinning broadly. He crossed the room to her and offered his hand. "Hi, I'm Randy Taylor. I'm the reasonable one. And you've already met Ian Russell, my not-so-silent partner."

Ian's scowl deepened as he rose to his feet and yanked off the makeup apron. He towered over the woman who'd just dusted him with something. "Look, you'll be better off talking to Randy on your show. I don't know about the 'more reasonable' part, but he's the more talkative one."

Randy laughed, shaking his head. "He's right. He's as talkative as a tree when he gets into a mood."

Dakota smiled, remembering an old Broadway song she'd heard in a recent revival. It was from *Paint Your Wagon* and entitled, "I Talk to the Trees." Suddenly she found herself wanting to talk to the trees.

Chapter Two

Moments before show time, Dakota gave her reluctant guest her brightest, ten-thousand-volt smile as she looked up into his stony face. "I'm sure you'll be fine."

As she assured him, she casually slipped her arm through his. She slowly began to stroll in the general direction of the soundstage as if it was the one true destination for them all.

It took a great deal of self-control for Ian not to snort at her remark. He was just as sure that he wouldn't be fine at all, and he at least had a basis for the opinion. He knew himself a hell of a lot better than this blond woman with the electric-blue eyes did.

This was all Taylor's fault, he thought, annoyed that

he'd allowed himself to be roped into this fiasco. Taylor was the one who had pushed for the appearance, claiming they could use the publicity that the syndicated talk show would bring them. Taylor was always in a rush.

He wasn't. As far as *he* was concerned, things were going fine just as they were. It took time to build up a decent clientele. Word of mouth was what did it—words from satisfied customers. A prolonged sound bite wouldn't ensure success.

Ian didn't bother suppressing his frown as he allowed himself to be steered. He saw no purpose in making an appearance on a program like some sideshow clown, having a bunch of strangers stare at him and pass judgment. The audience wouldn't care about his and Taylor's credentials. They wanted sensational entertainment.

That kind of thing didn't matter in the bodyguard business. Nor did it reflect the hard work he and Randy did every day.

Ian blew out a deep breath. He really regretted letting Taylor have his way in this. Even if the beautiful talk-show host did smell of something seductively floral and mind bending.

Randy inclined his head toward MacKenzie as they followed his partner and Dakota. It took a bit of doing, given that there was almost a foot between them. "She's good."

MacKenzie took great pride in compliments sent Dakota's way. They were a team, she and Dakota, and each reveled in the other's good fortune. It was she who had first suggested to Dakota that she become a talk-show hostess. If ever there was a natural for this kind of format, it was Dakota.

She flashed a smile at the good-looking man on her left. "You don't know the half of it. If she set her mind to it Dakota could get the sphinx to talk and reveal its secrets."

Which was exactly what made Dakota Delany such a hugely successful talk-show host. Her audience had multiplied exponentially since her debut four years ago. Friends called just to tell one another about it. Soon, everyone was tuning in, wanting to know what the party was all about. Her fans were legion.

MacKenzie firmly believed that her friend had the kind of face people talked to, a manner that almost verbally declared that she could be trusted. And why not? With her easy laugh and quick wit, Dakota reminded people of their sister, their mother, their best friend or a favorite aunt, someone they could turn to in both good times and bad.

It wasn't so much the way Dakota looked—which was gorgeous with a capital *G*—as it was her manner. She seemed genuinely interested in whatever was being said to her, whether a guest was trying to explain medical science's latest attempts to cure a major disease, or some Hollywood star expounding on his or her most recent misadventures. Dakota would always manage to get to the heart of the matter and extract the one thing that would make her audience sit up and take notice. Make them feel as if they were right there with her in the simple living room setting she'd made as her center stage.

Every weekday at two o'clock, her audience felt as if they were being invited into her home for a friendly chat. With good reason. Dakota made sure that the soundstage where they taped looked exactly like her own living room. Being at ease herself was the first step toward getting a good interview.

MacKenzie watched her friend work her magic on the day's reluctant guest.

If the man beside her were any stiffer, he would have been a tree, Dakota thought. She could feel him champing at the bit to get out of there. She'd interviewed and talked to enough people to know that this man was not exactly a willing guest. She suspected that his partner had everything to do with their appearance on the show.

Well, it didn't matter how he had gotten here, it was up to her to make him feel at ease. Or as much at ease as a man like Ian Russell could be.

Rising up slightly on her toes, ignoring the fact that MacKenzie and Randy Taylor were right behind her, Dakota brought her lips close to Ian's ear. "This isn't going to hurt, Ian, I give you my word."

The woman's warm breath swirled around his ear, forging a path along his neck and traveling the short distance to his chin. Rather than calm him, the simple act succeeded in creating a sensual riot that ran amok through his system.

Unaccustomed to being the one who needed to be assured of anything, Ian pulled back to look at her. "What?" he demanded sharply.

"The interview," Dakota explained quietly, never taking her eyes from his. "It's painless. And it'll be over with before you know it."

He really doubted that. He'd once been on a five-day stakeout, living in his car and subsisting on cold burgers and colder fries. Right now that seemed like a day at the amusement park in comparison to the way he felt about the next twenty minutes.

Ian slanted a look toward the woman whose parents had named her after two states. Obviously they were one sandwich short of a picnic basket, just as she was.

"We'll see," Ian muttered under his breath as they turned down the long corridor. He glanced at the photographs of celebrities hanging on either side and was completely unimpressed.

That we will, Dakota thought.

Reaching the perimeter of the soundstage where her show was taped, she saw that the crew had already assembled. Billy Webster, a comedian she'd seen at one of the local comedy clubs and liked instantly, was out in front of the curtain, warming up the audience for her. He was nearing the end of his monologue.

That meant that they were going to be on the air in less than five minutes. Dakota glanced at the last-minute fill-in at her side. Standing ramrod straight, he looked even taller than he was. And more foreboding, if that was even possible. She needed this man to be more fluid, or at least in some kind of condition that didn't immediately bring Dutch elm disease to mind.

Usually, the touch of her hand and the warm look in her eyes was enough.

But not today.

Positioning herself so that he was forced to see only her, she tried again. "Look, the process is a lot easier if you forget about the audience and just talk to me," she coaxed. "Tell me why I'd want to hire your firm instead of some other. Most important, I want the audience to understand the difference between what you do and what they've seen in the movies."

"I get it. Kind of like reality TV," Randy interjected.

Her eyes shifted to Randy's face for a moment. "Something like that."

Instincts she'd been blessed with told her that she would undoubtedly have a better show, or at least a better chance of attaining one, if she directed her questions and the interview toward tree man's partner. Unless she missed her guess, Randy Taylor seemed to be a live wire, capable of talking the ears off an African elephant.

But she was her parents' stubborn daughter. Given a choice, she had never picked the easier way. If she had, she'd be lolling on some absurd flotation device in her parents' Beverly Hills pool, absorbing the California sun and letting life just drift by.

She lived for challenges, and right now the close-mouthed Ian Russell was her challenge. Besides, although both men were notably good-looking, it was Ian Russell who rightfully earned the label of tall, dark and handsome.

Dark. Dakota couldn't help wondering if that went clear down to his soul. From the look in his eyes, she was willing to bet that it did.

The show's director caught her eye and nodded. Which meant her introduction was coming. She gave the bodyguard's arm a quick squeeze.

"My cue's coming up," she said suddenly. "Zee will send you two out as soon as I announce your names." She paused to add, "Remember, this is going to be fun." With this, Dakota vanished from the small space, leaving him behind the curtain with Randy and the production assistant.

Ian frowned. It was obvious that he and the incredibly perky blonde had completely different definitions of the word fun. To be honest, he wasn't sure if he defined anything as fun. The absence of tension was good enough for him. And right now he wished he was in that state.

It annoyed him that he could feel his adrenaline kicking in. That was supposed to happen when he was faced with a fight-or-flight situation, not because he was going to be sitting on some overly warm soundstage, looking into the eyes of some motor-mouth talk-show hostess while he was waiting to be humiliated.

Actually, that had already happened. And it would only get worse.

He looked at his partner accusingly. "Don't know

why I let you talk me into this," he growled, his deep voice even lower.

Unfazed, Randy shook his head. "Because, at bottom you know I'm right."

"At bottom," Ian echoed. The soft buzz of the woman's voice floated backstage. He couldn't make out the words, only that the audience was laughing in response. His discomfort grew.

"Right now I'd rather be at the bottom of some lake than waiting to be stripped bare in front of—" he turned toward MacKenzie suddenly "—how big did you say that the audience was?"

Her expression told him that didn't think this was the time to repeat that particular statistic. She probably thought he'd get stage fright. If that was the case, she was dead wrong. It didn't matter to him if there was one person sitting out there or one million. The numbers didn't change the fact that he didn't like the prospect he was about to face.

"We need the publicity," Randy had insisted when he'd brought the idea to him. He'd presented it right after a week had passed with both of them staying at the office, waiting for the phone to ring. It didn't seem to matter to Randy that the week had come on the heels of three very hectic months where neither of them had had more than a day off at a time.

Even when they'd been on the force together, his partner's mind was always racing ahead, always thinking about the next case that would come their way. In a moment of weakness, Ian had given in to his partner about this show. Giving in to Randy was something he rarely did and never with this kind of consequence.

Makeup. He'd been asked to wear makeup, for pity's sake. He should have walked out then, leaving Randy holding the bag, instead of allowing that Delany woman to take over and actually apply some to his face. He didn't care what the reasons were, a man's face was not made to have makeup on it.

As if to reinforce his convictions, he could feel his skin growing itchy. Could feel himself growing itchy, as well. Itchy to get the hell out of here.

Ian turned on his heel, ready to put thought into action, only to find the little production assistant blocking his way. The look in her green eyes forbade him to move.

Like that could actually stop him, Ian thought. It would have taken no effort at all just to place his hands on her shoulders and lift her out of the way.

"Don't even think it," MacKenzie warned, digging the heels of her soft leather boots into the floor.

Ian's eyes narrowed even as he fought back a grin. He always admired displays of courage, even baseless courage. But before he could say anything to Dakota's second-in-command, he heard his name being called. Ian instinctively stiffened. The fledgling grin faded.

Taylor clapped his hand on his shoulder. "That's us, Russell."

Turning to look toward the set, Ian felt the little brunette's hands on the small of his back. The next moment she was pushing him in the direction of the set. Rather than take the lead the way he was so inclined to do, this time Randy fell into place behind him. Which meant that if he wanted to leave, he was going to have to send them both flying out of his way.

All right, so not today.

Muttering an oath about Taylor's not-so-distant lineage under his breath, Ian squared his shoulders and began to walk out toward the set.

The noise level seemed to grow with each step he took.

"You owe me, Taylor," he growled at his partner. "Big-time."

"We'll settle up later," Randy promised through lips that barely moved. The next moment he smiled broadly. "Smile, damn it, Ian," Randy hissed. "We're not exactly walking out to face a firing squad."

"Might as well be."

Stoically Ian pushed back the curtain and walked out, blinking as he tried to accustom his eyes to the bright lights. He forced himself to endure this and made an effort to change his expression. He wasn't about to become some grinning hyena. But he knew that if he continued to look as somber as he felt, not only would business *not* grow, it might even drop off.

Dakota deliberately made eye contact with the taller of the two men, smiling warmly and willing him to loosen up. He looked as if he expected her to start poking at him with a hot branding iron.

"And here they are now, folks." Placing herself temporarily between the two men, she escorted them the final ten steps to the set.

An arm hooked through each of theirs, Dakota nodded first to the right. "I want you to meet Ian Russell," she said warmly, then nodded to the left, "and Randy Taylor, the two men who pooled their considerable abilities to form Bodyguard, Inc." Gesturing for the men to take a seat on the cream-colored Italian leather sofa, she sat down on the overstuffed armchair that faced them. Only then did she glance toward her audience. "Not a very flashy name, I know, but it gets its message across, and I'm a firm believer that sometimes simple is best."

The woman probably wouldn't know simple if it bit her, Ian thought. Because of the nature of his work, he was more than passingly acquainted with celebrity types. The moment any kind of fame came their way, they lost all perspective, became little demigod dictators without any sense of reality. Opulence became their king, not simplicity.

"What these men provide," Dakota was telling her audience, "is a very basic service." A chuckle rose from the middle of the crowd, swelling and working its way to the outer perimeter until it seemed to encompass most of the room. "Okay, minds out of the gutter, people," Dakota instructed with a laugh. "It's not *that* kind of service." Although, she could see why her audience, comprised predominantly of women, would think so, given the men they were ogling at. "It's protection. These men are modern-day white knights. Ian," she said, suddenly turning toward him, "why would I come to you?"

"What?"

He'd allowed his mind to wander, and Dakota had caught him completely off guard with her question. He'd been convinced that for the most part, since she appeared to be a savvy-looking woman, the talk-show hostess would know to focus her attention on and direct her questions to Taylor. Anyone could see that his partner was obviously the more gregarious of the two. Scratch that. "More" had nothing to do with it. He was the *only* gregarious one of the two of them.

Maybe Ms. Dakota Delany wasn't as savvy as he thought she was.

Dakota shifted in her seat, her body language telling him that despite his hesitation, she wasn't backing off. Her attention was completely focused on him.

Damn you, Taylor, he thought, hating the trapped feeling that threatened to possess him.

"There are a lot of other companies out there," she persisted, her blue eyes never leaving his face. "Companies that are more established than yours. They all offer bodyguard service—something," she said in an aside to the audience, adding a familiar wink, "that I would personally never avail myself of." Her audience must be aware she had an aversion to having a paid-for shadow following her every move. She looked back at Ian. "Why come to you?"

His eyes met hers dead-on, letting her know he didn't

appreciate being placed on the spot. He was here as a silent support, a nonverbal backup. He wasn't the firm's spokesperson. "Because we'll get the job done," he told her simply.

Randy finally rode to the rescue. "Between us we've got fifteen years of experience on the force," he interjected. "And we know the kind of precautions that need to be taken."

Dakota glanced at the silver clipboard MacKenzie had shoved into her hands at the last minute. Typed notes in neat, short paragraphs summarized the men and their firm. Already familiar with what was written there, she looked only to reinforce herself.

"That's right, both of you are former homicide detectives." Turning toward the audience, she winked and said in her intimate way, "I do believe I feel safer already."

If Ian was hoping to catch a respite, the next moment found him disappointed. Dakota's attention was back on him.

"Being a former homicide detective makes you more familiar with the criminal mind than the average bodyguard might be." She leaned into him, effectively blocking out the audience and making this a conversation between the two of them. "Tell me, why did you leave the force?"

Randy was ready for this one. He had a pat answer all prepared, dealing with their wanting to grow as people, with their feeling that it was time to strike out on their own, etcetera.

But just as he opened his mouth to reply, Ian was the one who replied, "Too much paperwork."

Delighted by the honesty, the studio audience roared in response.

The laughter surprised Ian. He hadn't expected this kind of reaction. He certainly hadn't said it to be clever. He'd said it because it was true. Too much paperwork and too much red tape had driven him and then Taylor away from NYPD. There were too many rules to follow, and in his opinion a great many of them got in the way of doing decent police work.

Some of the other rules were just too damn frustrating. He'd seen too many bad guys go free on technicalities. So much so that one day, he, the son of a cop and the grandson of a cop, didn't want to be part of that system anymore.

Protecting people, men, women, and especially children, from any impending dangers meant something. He felt it made a difference. Enough of a difference for him to change what he'd thought was his life's calling in order to form this partnership with Taylor.

Actually, the company had been Taylor's idea, fashioned one lazy, sweltering-hot New York summer afternoon as they sat in O'Hara's, nursing two well-deserved beers.

The moment the suggestion had come out of Taylor's mouth, he remembered taking to it wholeheartedly. Ian knew that Taylor had espoused the idea because he felt that there was a great deal of money to be made, protecting the rich and famous. His own reasons were different. He'd taken to it because, the way he saw it, there was a difference to be made. Even the rich and famous deserved to be free of fear.

The laughter died down. Ian wasn't following up his words so Dakota pushed a little bit more, hoping to get the reluctant guest to speak on his own volition. She had a feeling that once this man finally became vocal, he would have things to say that were worth hearing.

"Any other reason than your dislike of putting things down on paper?" she asked innocently.

Ian realized that just for the tiniest slice of a second, he'd gotten lost in her eyes, lost in her expression. Had to be the hot lights. They were all over the place and so intense they could make a grown man dizzy if he wasn't careful.

"Yeah, I like keeping people safe."

The smile Dakota gave him in response to his answer made him feel as if warm butter flowed in his veins.

Reorienting himself to the immediate situation, he glanced at his watch. Only three minutes had gone by. That meant there were seventeen more minutes to endure, seventeen more minutes pregnant with sixty seconds apiece.

Eternity loomed before him like a dark specter.

Suppressing a groan, he sincerely began to miss his stakeout days.

Chapter Three

Dakota knew in her bones that the segment would be good.

She knew if she could just move her less-than-talkative guest in the right direction, the audience would meet him more than halfway. Once that was accomplished, this portion of her program would be off and flying.

She did what she could to make it happen.

Rather than ask what the audience could do to protect themselves against a potential stalker, Dakota had given her question a more personal ring by asking what *he,* Ian Russell, would do to protect a woman who came to him seeking help. As he cleared his throat, a hush fell over her normally boisterous audience. It was as if every woman there was hanging on his every word, probably envisioning herself as a damsel in distress being rescued by this modern-day Galahad.

Everyone loved this kind of fantasy. Dakota was counting on it.

Ian didn't disappoint her.

Even though his response was mostly technical, it was enough to arouse the imaginations of the women in the audience. Randy was quick to chime in, augmenting points here and there, adding layers to the audience's daydream. And it didn't hurt any to have the two men casually mention successfully foiling a kidnapping attempt of one of their clients.

As she listened, the details had a very familiar ring. Her eyes widened.

"That was Rebecca Anderson," Dakota suddenly realized out loud. Six months ago the story about the A-list actress and her would-be kidnapper had made all the major papers, not to mention the rounds of evening tabloid TV. "You two were responsible for saving her?" How could she have missed something like that? Dakota upbraided herself silently.

"Actually, Ian was." Randy looked at his partner with the kind of pride that only the closest camaraderie bred.

Well, that explained why she didn't know, Dakota thought. The man probably vanished at the first sign of a reporter, like any superhero caught slipping into his secret identity.

Dakota looked at the man on the sofa, no small amount of admiration flooding through her veins. She recalled that the kidnapper had been a burly, giant of a man who must have had seventy pounds and five inches on Ian. The lightest thing about the stalker had been his mind, which had clearly taken a holiday when it came to the subject of the glamorous Rebecca Anderson. When the police took him away, he was screaming that Rebecca was his wife, that she'd promised undying love to him and he was going to see to it that she never looked at another man ever again.

Dakota leaned into Ian and asked in a stage whisper, "Want to talk about it some more?"

If there was a man who was less uncomfortable than Ian Russell at this moment, she would gladly have paid for his passage to oblivion.

"No," Ian replied.

"Okay then, it's time for questions and answers," she glibly informed her audience.

The moment the words were out of her mouth, a veritable sea of hands shot up, all waving madly to catch her attention. Dakota didn't recall ever having seen so many hands raised as she did this afternoon. Delighted, she got started, selecting women at random.

Ten minutes later there was no indication that the questions were going to abate in the near future. Addressing questions to both men, the audience was leaning sixty-forty toward Ian.

Dakota briefly debated terminating the segment, then

decided to go for it and let it continue. When you had a hit on your hands, you just kept going. Wasn't that something her grandfather had once taught her? So, Dakota "just kept going."

It was evident to her that the last-minute interview would go down as one of her best. There was no doubt in her mind that the segment was an unqualified hit.

As it ran over its allotted time slot, Dakota made a quick decision to ask Joe Lansing, their musical guest, to return the next day in order to showcase his new CD. A twenty-year veteran of the business, Lansing was far too much of a professional not to know that when you found yourself holding lightning in a bottle, you didn't set it down.

Other than pointing to various waving hands, Dakota mostly kept her silence, letting Randy and, on occasion, Ian answer the questions. Her audience appeared to be in seventh heaven. Which placed her there as well.

She'd never had an hour slip by so effortlessly, so quickly.

Even as the strains of her theme song began to weave themselves through the air, the audience gave no sign of being sated.

But all good things had to end, and her program would be over in less time than it took to say it. Time to wind things up.

She rose from her seat, immediately followed by the two men.

"All right, ladies, Ian and Randy have to get back to

doing what they do best." She beamed at the two men. Randy was grinning from ear to ear while Ian looked just the slightest bit befuddled. Funny, she wouldn't have thought anything could have accomplished that. The man seemed far too on top of things for that to have happened. "Maybe we can persuade you two to come back sometime."

Before either could answer, the audience cheered and chimed a resounding "Yes" in response.

Dakota laughed. "I guess that settles it, then." Out of the corner of her eye she saw the director signal her. She gave a slight inclination of her head then looked toward the main camera. "This is Dakota Delany, thanking you for tuning in. Come by tomorrow so that I can get in another word edgewise."

She winked, knowing that the camera was fading to the credits.

"And it's a wrap," the director declared, crossing to them.

Dakota looked to the wings where her own security people had converged. "Looks like the bodyguards just might need bodyguards to make their way off the stage," she quipped.

"We finally through?" Ian asked. He didn't bother hiding the impatient edge that had slipped into his voice. When she nodded, she suddenly felt him place his arm about her waist and abruptly guide her toward the rear. She half expected him to keep on moving once they reached backstage, but then his arm slipped away. An odd sort of regret filtered through her but she dismissed it in the next moment.

Behind her she could have sworn that she heard some of the audience audibly sighing. She became aware that Ian was watching her with more than a hint of an accusation in his eyes. Obviously this hadn't been as good an experience for him as it had been for Randy or the audience.

"I thought your assistant said the segment was only going to be twenty minutes long."

Dakota raised one shoulder, letting it drop casually. "Ordinarily it is. On the average, we fit in three guests every hour. But you two were an unqualified hit." She grinned at both of them, but only Randy responded. "In the four years I've been doing this, I've never seen an audience take to guests the way they did to you two."

Randy's eyes were all but gleaming. With a barely concealed whoop, he looked at Ian. "Business is going to be booming," he predicted.

Dakota nodded. "I'm sure it will be. You might even have to hire extra people."

Ian shook his head. "I really doubt if any of those women in the audience are going to need a bodyguard in the near future."

Her eyes met his. "You never know. As you pointed out, it's not just celebrities who have stalkers. Regular people are plagued by them, as well."

MacKenzie sailed up to join them, her feet barely touching the floor. She'd witnessed the show inside the production booth, having full advantage of all the cameras trained on the set.

"That was wonderful," she enthused. She grabbed hold of Dakota's hands. "Could you just feel all that energy out there?"

"Feel it?" Dakota laughed. "A couple of times I thought it was going to swallow us up."

As far as Dakota was concerned, this was almost the best part of the show—the aftermath when, if the show was a particularly successful one, the energy level surged almost through the roof. She felt far too charged to retreat into her dressing room to go over the next day's show.

She glanced at Randy and saw that the man was making more than a little eye contact with her production assistant. Maybe this could use a little nurturing. She tried to remember the last time MacKenzie had mentioned going out with someone. Nothing came to mind. Her friend needed to get out.

"Listen," she said suddenly, placing her hand on Randy's wrist to get his attention, "do you two have to rush off just yet?"

Randy avoided looking in Ian's direction, as if he knew a contradiction was in the offing. "Not particularly."

"Good." Dakota's smile took in both men and her best friend. "Why don't the two of you join Mac and me for a drink—or whatever?"

One dark eyebrow rose in a quizzical crescent. "Whatever?" Ian echoed.

Dakota played back her own words. Oh God, did he think she was propositioning him? Her voice as smooth as silk, she was quick to clarify the potential misunderstanding. "Early dinner, late lunch, whatever you feel like having."

Ian shifted his weight. The backstage area was quickly filling up with people whose jobs he couldn't begin to guess at. That created a very small space for the four of them to occupy.

Most especially, for the two of them, he thought darkly. The bubbly woman could have been his shadow, or at least an extension of him, she was standing so close. Close enough for him to feel her breathing. Close enough for the scent she was wearing to infiltrate his senses. Consequently, when she ended her offer by saying "whatever you feel like having" he found himself thinking that he felt like having her.

The thought surprised him. He took a second to get his bearings and himself under control. He was a great believer in instinct, and right now instinct told him that Dakota Delany was the type that if you gave her an inch, she found a way to turn it into a town.

There was no way he was about to get socially mixed up with someone like that. Or anyone else for that matter. He was still one of the walking wounded as far as romance was concerned. He'd learned the hard way that he wasn't cut out for relationships. There were ways of satisfying sexual urges without getting sucked into a situation that required talking afterwards, or even interaction—both of which he preferred to avoid if at all possible. With everyone.

The best way was to beg off at the very beginning. "No, I don't—"

He felt Randy's hand suddenly on his shoulder. "We'd love it," Randy declared firmly. "Wouldn't we, Ian?"

Trapped, Ian shrugged dismissively. "Yeah, love it," he echoed.

Dakota noticed how the look on Ian's face was akin to thunderclouds descending over the plains. But she felt too good to allow him to dampen her mood. On a whim, she decided to bring him around, just as she had on the show.

"Well, that was certainly a resounding positive vote." She laughed as she threaded her arm through Ian's, beginning to forge a path for them. "C'mon, I know a great place to go. We can walk there."

A slight din began to come from the front of the stage. It seemed that security hadn't managed to clear away their audience just yet.

MacKenzie fell quickly in behind Dakota. "I suggest walking fast," she told the group, "before the audience decides to make a break for it and cut us off."

The people around them parted, but only enough to allow them to wiggle through. Acutely aware that his arm was still in Dakota's possession, Ian glanced over his shoulder toward the stage as they made their way out.

"I had no idea women could be that, um—" He paused, searching for a word that wouldn't ultimately be offensive, then finally settled on "pushy."

Dakota caught her tongue between her teeth to keep from laughing. So, despite his somewhat gruff demeanor, the man could be innocent, as well. She had to admit she found it rather refreshing.

"You'd be surprised," she said before turning back to the task of getting them out of the studio.

He was trying not to be, Ian thought, attempting not to notice the way her hips swayed as she pulled out in front of him. He was definitely trying not to be.

Heaven, Dakota's restaurant of choice that night, was located only three blocks from the studio where her program was taped. In the last four years Heaven had become a home away from home to her. Certainly the food there was better than anything that could be found in her own kitchen.

Today, as always, Heaven was fairly humming with patrons, both regulars and first-timers. An elegantly decorated restaurant, its walls were lined with photographs of celebrities who frequented the premises. As on any other day, several could be spotted seated at the scattered tables and booths, enjoying the fare.

It was damn crowded, Ian noted. The line they'd just circumvented was clear out the door. He didn't take Dakota for the type to cut in front of people, which meant that he was off the hook. "I guess we came at the wrong time," he said to Dakota.

About to retreat, he found his path impeded by the effervescent woman.

"Not so fast," she told him as she turned to the maître d'. Dakota greeted the man and subsequently was embraced in what amounted to a Russian bear hug.

Ian sighed. Looked as if he'd failed to factor in the magic of star power.

The tall, mustached man in the dark suit smiled broadly as he released Dakota. "For you? How could there not be a table for you, my friend? Always, always there will be a place for you and your friends anywhere I will be," he swore, dramatically hitting his chest with his fist.

Dakota inclined her head with a smile. "Thank you, Dimitri."

The aristocratic man looked around for a waiter. Spying one, he was quick to dispatch the man into the center of the dining area. Within two minutes Dakota and the others were ushered to a booth that was off to the side.

The tables around them were filled to capacity with people who clearly enjoyed themselves and their meals. It seemed rather improbable to Ian that this plum location had gone begging all this time. He looked at Dakota as the waiter distributed elegant black menus with gold lettering. "He kill the people who were sitting here?"

"You always view everything so darkly?" Dakota asked.

He shrugged absently. "Just seems surprising that with all these people in here and that line at the door, that this booth would go empty and unnoticed."

"It doesn't, exactly." She paused to order a bottle of

wine for the table, then looked back at Ian. "Dimitri keeps it reserved for me."

That didn't seem like a sound business move, unless there was something going on between her and the silver-haired man. The embrace had seemed particularly warm and friendly.

"What else does he keep reserved for you?"

"The best wine in the house," she answered glibly, nodding at the departing waiter. She deliberately took no offense, sensing he didn't mean it as an insult but more of a probe.

Ian's gray eyes held hers. He had no idea what prompted him to ask, "What do you do in exchange for all this service?"

Randy leaned in, an apologetic expression on his lean face. "You'll have to excuse my partner. He left his brain in his other skull."

Dakota took it all in stride. "Along with his manners, I guess. Glad they lasted the length of the show."

She should have left it there, she told herself. After all, the man had no right to infer anything. But she wanted to set the record straight.

"And to answer your question, this is Dimitri's way of showing his gratitude. This place is his first restaurant in this country. I had him on my very first show and sent a little business his way as he was starting out. His excellent menu and fantastic culinary skill—until recently, he was the head chef, as well—did the rest. But he still chooses to be grateful, and I do like the food here." Finished, she gave him an inquiring look. "Any other questions?"

Ian laughed shortly. He supposed he had that coming. He had no idea why he'd pushed the issue, only that an uncustomary flare of temper had surfaced when he saw the way the older man had held on to Dakota for a beat too long. There was no reason why he should have cared, even if the two were lovers.

"I guess that puts me in my place. Sorry."

Randy almost choked on the water he'd just sipped. Regaining control, he stared at Ian. "Oh God, this is a monumental moment. Russell never apologizes."

Ian opened the menu, hoping to return to business as usual. The selections ran down two long columns. "Because I'm usually not wrong."

Randy grinned. "He's also been known to walk on water on occasion."

MacKenzie's eyes shifted to the other man. "Now *that* I'd like to book for the show."

Ian didn't even glance up. "Sorry, only private showings."

Dakota laughed. Her eyes fairly gleamed with delight as she looked at him. "Hey, you do have a sense of humor."

"Sometimes," he muttered, wishing his partner would start to use his gift of gab and bail him out of this.

As if sensing Ian's thoughts and taking pity on him, Randy picked up the menu and looked down the long columns. "So, what's good here?"

"I can honestly say everything," Dakota told him. MacKenzie nodded her assent. "I've sampled every item at one time or another and couldn't tell you which was his best."

Ian glanced over the top of his menu. His eyes slowly slid down as much of her trim torso as was visible to him. Women didn't generally admit to having a healthy appetite, so he believed her. "How do you keep the weight off?"

Dakota thought for a moment. Weight had never been a problem for her. "Regular exercise, I suppose." Or as regular as she could get it, given her hectic schedule.

"Having the metabolism of a hummingbird doesn't hurt, either," MacKenzie chimed in.

Dakota laughed. "You should talk." If she were into envying people, MacKenzie would be at the top of her list. The smaller woman could eat from morning until night and never show any of it. "She eats ice cream as if it was going out of style and never gains so much as a lousy ounce."

Ian smiled politely at both women. He was here to have a drink and a late lunch, nothing more. He'd managed to keep a distance between himself and the people he worked for. Doing the same with Dakota Delany shouldn't be difficult.

Shouldn't be, a small voice in his mind echoed for reinforcement.

The small voice somehow rang false.

Ian closed his menu as the food server came their

way to take their order. He glanced at the glass of wine standing by his plate. He'd never really cared for wine. "They have beer here?"

Dakota grinned. "More kinds than you could possibly imagine."

Maybe this wasn't going to be so bad after all, he thought. He raised his eyes to Dakota's.

Then again...

Chapter Four

The buzzing pulsed insistently as it wedged its way into a low-grade din in the restaurant.

MacKenzie sighed, retiring her menu to the table. She looked up at their slim-hipped food server who stood with an electronic pad and stylus poised in his hand.

"I'm probably going to have to pass," she said. Tilting the pager that had become a permanent accessory, she nodded. "Yup, I'm going to have to pass." She exchanged looks with Randy. "The studio's paging me."

"Why don't you just call them back?" Randy asked.

Both Dakota and she knew that it was never that simple. "A—" she held up one finger "—the reception here's usually not the best. Like as not, I'll probably pick up Angela Redding's conversation." Underscoring her point, MacKenzie nodded at a mature-looking woman sitting at the next table. The woman's autographed photo graced the wall and she was known as the grande dame of one of the longest-running soap operas on the air. "And B—" a second finger joined the first "—they'll just tell me to get back there, anyway."

Randy rose to his feet to let her slide out of the booth. MacKenzie flashed a smile at Ian and Randy. "It's been fun," she told the two men.

Randy stopped her before she could leave. "Why don't I walk you back?"

The suggestion freshened her smile, but etiquette had her protesting. "You don't have to do that."

Randy gave a half shrug. "Well, since I'm on my feet anyway," he pointed out, "I might as well just keep moving." He took her arm. "Besides, this gives me a chance to ask a few questions."

Dakota noted that her friend gave up any attempt at protest. "Is charm part of being a bodyguard?"

"It helps." He looked over his shoulder at Ian. "I'll catch up with you later." Ian merely nodded. Randy inclined his head toward the other occupant of the booth. "Dakota, a pleasure."

"Likewise."

She watched Randy and MacKenzie leave. Was it her imagination, or did their bodies appear to be closer than the space around them necessitated? Maybe this was the start of something good for MacKenzie. The woman had no social life outside of the show.

Neither do you anymore.

And it was going to stay that way, she decided firmly. Getting burned once was enough for her, at least until the next century. Clearing her throat, she looked back at the man beside her in the booth. "So, is stoicism the other part of being a bodyguard?"

He ignored her question. Without Randy as a buffer, it was going to get painfully quiet at the table. Taking the initiative, he slid to the edge of the booth. "Look, we don't have to stay."

But Dakota made no move to follow him out. Instead, she placed her hand on his wrist. "Sure we do. We're the only ones who've placed their orders."

That stopped him for a moment. "I'm not much on conversation."

"That's okay. I am." Mildly certain that she'd snuffed out his inclination to go, she took her hand from his wrist. "My father used to say I talked more than any three people he knew."

"Sounds like a sharp man."

There was nothing she liked better than to talk about her family. A warm smile curved her mouth. "He is. He does the evening news on Channel Seven."

Most people she met already knew that, since Daniel Delany had been in the business for over thirty years and had been coming into people's living rooms, delivering the news in one form or another. But she had a feeling that Ian Russell was not "most people." More than likely, whatever didn't touch his immediate sphere didn't merit his interest.

"His name is Daniel Delany," she added. As she watched, she thought she saw a vague spark of recognition filter through his eyes.

He did follow the news, although he paid little attention to the perfectly groomed parade of newscasters who delivered it. After taking a long drink from the glass of beer, he finally acknowledged, "Name's familiar."

She'd never met a living man without a pulse before, she thought. Still, there was an undercurrent of magnetism that transcended his less-than-lively delivery. Maybe it was the soft lighting, but he seemed to smolder.

As if the proximity suddenly struck him as too close, Ian abruptly moved his place setting to the other side of the table so that they would face each other.

About to protest his sudden rise to his feet, she realized that he was only seeking the shelter of distance and not leaving. Did she make him that uncomfortable? "I'll tell him you said that the next time I talk to him," she said.

He nodded, hunting for some kind of response. He didn't want her thinking he was a stone statue, although he'd already warned her about that, and besides, it should have made no difference what she thought.

Still, because the atmosphere threatened to fill up with dead air, he asked what he thought was the obvious. "Stay in touch much? With your father?" he asked.

"As much as I can." She broke a bread stick, nibbling

on one end. She hadn't realized that she was as hungry as she was. The urge for an unscheduled pilgrimage to the land of used, overpriced possessions had come before she'd had anything for breakfast. She counted herself lucky that her stomach hadn't rumbled. "My parents live on the West Coast. California," she added.

West Coast and California were synonymous to her, but that was only because she'd grown up there. Everyone always felt that their home was the epicenter of everyone's focus, she mused just as the food server returned with their orders.

"Fast," Ian commented in a low voice.

"They like to keep things moving here," she said as she dug into her food with unabashed relish. "Dimitri's thinking of buying out the store next door and expanding." He made no comment on the information. Big surprise. Dakota retreated to the previous topic. Her family. "My mother's Joanna Montgomery." Watching his expression, she saw no sign that the name might have meant something to him. *Sorry, Mom, not everyone's a movie buff.* "She's an actress."

He raised one eyebrow at the information. His late mother had been a homemaker, struggling to create harmony between two men who had nothing in common aside from their surname and choice of profession. She was the rock of the earth. Actresses, he felt, were the complete opposite. "Your whole family is in show business?"

"My older brother, Paul, is an accountant." She didn't bother adding that he worked for a major studio.

Ian nodded. "Good for him."

There was something about the tone that rubbed her against the grain. She silently took offense for both her mother and her father. "But my grandfather's in the business," she informed him. "Waylon Montgomery."

Her almost-silent eating companion's head jerked up. By the surprised look on his face, Dakota knew she'd hit pay dirt. So the man did watch television. A sliver of triumph worked its way forward.

Ian's fork was suspended in midair. "You're kidding."

"It's in my official bio," she deadpanned.

"Savage Ben's owner is your grandfather?" Ian asked. Savage Ben had been a cult favorite TV program in the early eighties and was still living happily in reruns around the world.

He couldn't believe it. Waylon Montgomery had a face that had been lived in years before his hair had turned white. Not that he'd ever given the matter any thought, but if he had, he would have imagined that the man would have fathered rather homely children, not someone who took men's breath away in a wheelbarrow.

"One and the same." Impulse put the words in her mouth. "He's coming out at the end of the month to do an interview. I could arrange for you to meet him if you like."

"I—my son and I used to watch that on Saturday mornings together." The last thing he wanted was for her to think of him as one of those people without a life, who faithfully attached themselves to celebrities and went out of their way to see them.

The piece of personal information took her by surprise. So did the strange pang she felt.

The man was married.

That didn't matter, she silently insisted.

Dakota forced herself to focus on what he'd just said. Maybe Ian Russell was warming up to her. Or maybe finding out who her grandfather was had momentarily shaken up his world.

"And then what?" she coaxed, trying to get him to continue. "He outgrew it?" Kids were rebelling and trying to act cool sooner these days. She'd never gone through a rebellion herself, but all her friends had. She'd been in the minority.

Ian looked back at his plate as he resumed eating. "I wouldn't know."

There was something about the set of his shoulders that got to her. She paused a moment, wondering if she should hold her tongue. But then, that had never stopped her before. "You're divorced, aren't you?"

Ian looked at her. He wanted to tell her that she had no right to probe, but curiosity got the better of him. "Does it show?"

"In a manner of speaking," she allowed. "You don't strike me as the type to suddenly ignore your son. Something else had to have happened. Divorce was my first guess." Mostly because so many people she knew found themselves in that position at one time or another. That she hadn't had one marriage to her name made her unusual. "They say fifty percent of the couples wind up that way."

His expression was dour. "Nice to know I didn't mess up any statistics."

She forgot about being hungry. Dakota leaned her head against her hand. "What happened?"

The look in his eyes warned her off. There was a DO NOT TRESPASS sign right there in big, bold letters. She ignored it.

"A little personal, don't you think?" He all but growled the words.

"Yes," she answered with unabashed honesty and enthusiasm. "But if we're going to be friends—"

The knife fell from his fingers, clattering to the plate. Ian looked at her sharply. "Who said we're going to be friends?"

"I did." And then she smiled at him. Ian found the smile completely unreadable. And annoying. As were her next words. "And, in a way, you did."

The woman was clearly suffering from some kind of delusions. "What?"

"Your partner left with my production assistant. You're still here."

He blew out a breath. Why was she making more out of this than there was? He'd remained because, after giving it some thought, it was logical to stay, nothing else.

"Like you pointed out, we'd already ordered. And I was hungry. No sense in letting good food go to waste."

He watched as a completely unfathomable smile played along her lips. "Whatever you say."

He shook his head. "Anyone ever tell you you can be irritating?"

"Yes," she freely admitted, then added, "but my pure heart usually gets them to cut me some slack." Her expression softened a little, becoming just a shade serious. "You don't have to tell me why you got divorced if you don't want to."

"Thanks," he said. He'd thought that was the end of it, but looking back, he should have known better. Gorgeous though she was, Dakota Delany still had something in common with an unrelenting freight train.

"But my guess would be that she got tired of being a cop's wife, tired of waiting to see if you'd come walking through that door each night."

She'd hit the nail right on the head on her first try. He supposed that made his life predictable. "Not very original, is it?"

"Doesn't have to be original to hurt."

If that was pity, he wanted no part of it. "You always probe people like this over a meal?"

"No. Sometimes I do it over drinks."

She got the smile she was after. Granted, it was just the barest hint of a smile, but given the kind of person she was working with, she figured it was a major triumph. Dakota saw his eyes shift to just beneath her chin. He was either contemplating clipping her one, or her necklace had caught his eye.

"It's a cameo," she said, watching his eyes as he admired her necklace.

"Family heirloom?"

She'd made short work of her meal, she realized. Taking the last bite, she placed her fork down on the plate and crossed her knife over it.

"Somebody's family," she allowed, "but not mine. I just bought it this morning at one of those quaint little stores along the coast." She thought about it for a moment. Funny how that had fallen into place for her. Her mother was the one who adored antiques. As a child, she'd always thought of haunting the various dusty little stores as punishment. Maybe something inside of her had wanted to retreat to those childhood days, where there had been parents to buffer her and keep hurt from her door. "Don't even know why I went. I don't usually go to those kinds of stores." There were a number of antique stores in the city and she only frequented those when her mother came to visit and to shop. "Certainly not if it requires getting behind a wheel and driving to them." Fingering the cameo again, she felt that same sort of restlessness taking hold that she'd felt this morning. She looked at Ian. "If I was the kind who believed in fate and destiny, I'd say it was almost as if I was supposed to find this cameo."

He snorted. "Sounds like a good credit card commercial."

"No, I'm serious." For some reason his dismissive expression made her defensive. "There's a legend that goes with this cameo."

A legend probably woven by some enterprising shop owner, he thought. "Oh?"

"The cameo belonged to an Amanda Deveaux during the Civil War. Her fiancé gave it to her just before he went off to fight. He told her not to take it off until he came back to marry her."

And she bought it, lock, stock, and barrel. He would have taken her for someone more savvy than that. "Let me guess, they buried her in it." He took a final sip of his beer. "Not a very cheery legend. Aren't you afraid that thing might carry a curse?"

It was obvious by his tone that he didn't believe in destiny, fate or curses. But then, neither did she. Normally. There'd just been something about this cameo when she'd looked at it…

She bit her lower lip, realizing that she'd never gotten the woman in the shop to tell her if Amanda's fiancé had ever returned. "I don't know if they buried her in it."

"You didn't ask? I thought you dissected everyone you came in contact with."

She took no offense at the clinical description. "I asked, but then she had this old grandfather clock there and it chimed. I realized I was going to be late for the program if I didn't get started back." She fingered the small oval as she rolled a thought over in her head. "I'm going to have to get back up there and ask her what happened." And have her on the show, she added silently. She looked at him. "There is more to the legend that she did tell me."

"And now you're going to tell me." Resignation echoed in his voice. "All right, what is it? If you kiss a frog while you're wearing it, he turns into a prince?"

She thought of saying something about trying that theory out by kissing him, but let the moment pass. She prided herself on not being the antagonistic type. "No, the wearer has true love enter her life."

This time, he did hoot. He hated seeing seemingly intelligent people taken. His mother had been like that. An eternal optimist who bought into every sob story that came her way. She was the softest touch in the neighborhood. His father had been the hardest.

"And you bought that?"

This time she did take offense. Dakota squared her shoulders. "No, I bought the necklace," she said deliberately, "because it was pretty. The last thing I am looking for is so-called true love."

He heard what she wasn't saying and studied her for a moment. Maybe things weren't quite so perfect in her world, either. "Sounds a little bitter."

A swell of hurt threatened to blanket her. She packed it away before it could get the better of her. John wasn't worth it, wasn't worth a single tear. Now that she looked back, she realized she really didn't love him, she loved the idea of him, the idea of love and having someone to love.

"Not bitter, realistic," she told Ian, then shrugged as she broke apart a bread stick she had no intention of eating, reducing it to minuscule crumbs. "People don't stay together the way they did in my parents' generation." Her voice became a little wistful, as well as sad. "Maybe it's because they don't love that way anymore."

There was something about her expression, about the look in her eyes that drew him in despite himself. "What way?"

"Undyingly. From the bottom of their toes." She dusted off her hands, then wiped her fingertips in her napkin. "Now it's a matter of boundaries and space and constantly looking out for yourself—"

If you didn't look out for yourself, he thought, you got cut down. "What's wrong with that?"

She didn't expect him to understand. But rather than retreat, passion swelled in her voice.

"It shouldn't be about maintaining your own space, it's supposed to be about melding, about looking out for your loved one, not yourself. Marriage takes work, it takes selflessness."

He leaned back and studied her. His ex would have called Dakota an embarrassment to her gender. Maybe the woman was deeper than he first thought. "That's definitely not women's lib."

Dakota frowned, waving a hand at his words. "I hate labels." She raised her chin like someone ready for a fight. "But if you want one, then fine, that's people lib." To her surprise, he laughed. She felt anger flaring. "Did I say something funny?"

"No, just unexpected." He supposed that was part of her appeal. She said the unexpected. If asked, he would have said that he had her pegged as a modern woman to the nth degree, interested in putting all men in their place. In his experience, women of privilege usually were.

The lighting played along her face, making him aware of her flawless complexion and incredible bone structure. Ian felt a vague, distant stirring and recognized it for what it was. Desire. He would have had to be a dead man not to notice that the woman was damn sexy. He would have had to have been a fool to act on it or think that any action might have led somewhere.

He turned his attention back to his meal. And to getting out of there in one piece.

The restlessness that had placed her behind the wheel of her BMW this morning refused to abate. Instead, as the minutes slipped by, it grew. Especially when Ian would look at her. She couldn't begin to guess what was going on in his mind, only that his eyes were making her warm.

The moment he finished, she signaled for the tab. When the food server arrived, she signed her name to the charge receipt that was already waiting for her.

"How much was that?" Ian asked, digging into his pocket for his wallet.

"Put that away," she told him. "You're not paying for this."

He did as she said, but he didn't like it. Maybe he was old-fashioned, but it went against his grain to allow a woman to pay for him. Even a woman he barely knew. "I'm not used to not paying."

"If we go out, you can pay," she told him flippantly as she slid out of the booth. "This, however, is on the show."

Damn, what the hell had made her say something like that? They weren't about to go out. Even though Ian had looked at her in a way that made her squirm inside, he certainly hadn't said or indicated that he was interested in making this personal. She doubted he knew *how* to make anything personal.

Shrugging, Ian placed a hand to the small of her back, escorting her out of the dining area and to the front of the restaurant. She looked back at Ian. The man did have his good points, she mused.

Once outside, Dakota noticed fallen leaves playing tag with the wind. She raised the collar of her jacket, thinking she should have brought a coat along.

Stepping toward the curb, Ian raised his hand at a passing cab. Its Off Duty sign not lit, the vehicle still flew right by him.

"I should have brought the car," he muttered. As she watched, Ian edged his way to the corner, waiting for the next cab.

One came less than a minute later. It pulled up right in front of them. Hand on the door, Ian turned to the woman who was standing at his side. She hadn't said anything for at least a minute. He wondered if he'd insulted her somehow.

"Well, thanks for lunch."

A smile played along her lips. "You're welcome. You did well."

"I've been eating on my own since before I was two."

She laughed, unaware that the sound filtered right into his system, increasing his discomfort. "I meant the show."

He was still unconvinced that his presence had been necessary. "Yeah, well, that would have gone better if Taylor had been your only guest."

She looked up into his face, her smile burrowing a small hole right into his gut. "Not from where I was sitting."

For a moment, as their eyes met, Dakota found herself holding her breath. She thought that he was going to kiss her. She realized that she wanted him to, even though they didn't know each other. There'd been an attraction building from the moment she'd taken the makeup brush and applied it to his cheekbones.

Get real, you're vulnerable because that two-faced liar cheated on you, nothing else.

The thought was sobering. She took a step back, hunching her shoulders against the chill in the air. "Maybe I'll see you around."

"Maybe," he acknowledged, folding his frame into the car.

And maybe not, she concluded silently as she watched the cab pull away from the curb and then merge into the midafternoon traffic.

The wind felt even chillier as she hurried back to the studio.

Chapter Five

As Dakota strode into the building, her mind was still on the man with whom she'd just shared lunch. Alan Curtis waylaid her the moment she entered the long corridor on the way to her dressing room. At six-three and 230 pounds, he wasn't someone she could easily circumvent. In the producer's rather wide shadow was MacKenzie, grinning from ear to ear. Since the other woman had left with Randy Taylor but he was nowhere to be seen, Dakota wasn't quite sure what to make of her friend's expression. She raised her brow silently in MacKenzie's direction, who just grinned wider, if that was possible.

"You're here!"

For a big man, Alan had a very high voice when he was excited, and he was clearly excited. Were they up for an award? Dakota wondered. She did a quick calculation and remembered that all the major awards were over for the year and it was too soon for the big nominations.

"Looks like it." Taking a few steps, she managed to get closer to her dressing room, but not by much. "Were you waiting for me?"

She usually went over the production notes for the next day's show after that day's taping was over, but it wasn't something she adhered to religiously. If Alan wanted to see her, he was being rather haphazard about it, she thought.

"Yes!" he declared with no less enthusiasm. His voice went up another octave.

"Then why didn't you page me?" It was obvious that he had to have been the one to page MacKenzie at the restaurant, and although she didn't wear her pager like a vital part of her body the way MacKenzie did, it was in her purse along with her cell phone. Neither had made a sound during her meal.

"Because I wanted you to finish having that late dinner with the bodyguard guy." The last time she'd seen Alan's eyes gleaming like this, he'd misread the directions on his eye drops and doubled the dosage.

"Oh-kay." Dakota drew out the word as she tried to fathom what the producer was talking about. The man wasn't in the matchmaking business, so what did it matter to him who she had lunch with and for how long? Unable to come up with a reason, she finally had to ask, "Why?"

"Because I want you two to have a rapport with each other."

Well, that certainly didn't clear anything up. She looked toward MacKenzie for some enlightenment. "Again, why?"

Impatient, MacKenzie jumped into the exchange, which was going nowhere. "The phones have been ringing off the hook."

Dakota tried to make some kind of sense out of the fragments she was being thrown. "Are they calling about the segment?"

"About the segment, about Russell and Taylor—" Alan began.

MacKenzie's eagerness got the better of her. It was obvious that whatever was going on, she took it to be a good thing. "And about what you said."

Dakota looked at her, confused. As far as she knew, she hadn't said anything extraordinary during the show. The unusual thing was that they had gone with just one segment and let it take over the entire program.

"I said a lot of things during the show, Zee, you're going to have to be a little more specific than that." Several people walked by, and she shifted out of the way. The miniparade temporarily separated her from Alan and MacKenzie.

Alan raised his voice to be heard above the other voices. "Let's go into your dressing room."

"I don't think I like the sound of that." Utterly curious now, she led the way into the room, closing the door as soon as the other two were in. She nodded at the chair before the vanity table. "Should I be sitting for this?" The question was addressed to Alan, but her eyes shifted toward MacKenzie for an answer.

Her friend ended the mystery. "Remember how you've said that you'd have a difficult time functioning with a bodyguard underfoot all the time, watching your back and parts thereof?"

It had begun as an off-the-cuff remark that had elicited laughter from the audience, just as she'd meant it to, even though her underlying feelings had been there. It had dovetailed into this segment rather well. Born a child of privilege, she didn't believe in entourages or in keeping an extended staff around her. She preferred her own company and to take care of any details that needed seeing to herself.

"Yes?" Her voice was wary as she waited for Mac-Kenzie to continue.

This time Alan cut in. "Well, your audience wants to see you deal with it."

"The audience?" she repeated, a slight thoughtful frown crossing her face. "You mean the people who were here today?" Had they taken some kind of an exit poll?

"No, your *audience*," he emphasized the last word. "The faithful followers who give up an hour of their life every day at two just to sit and watch you on the television. Eighty percent said they wanted you to have a bodyguard for a week or two and then get back to them with all the details." Alan looked immensely pleased. She could almost see him rubbing his hands together. "I guess they want to live vicariously."

She liked pleasing her audience, but there were limits. And she'd meant what she said about not liking the idea of having some stranger share her space, day in and day out. Dakota shook her head, her long hair moving back and forth like a blond storm.

"Not through me, not this way." She saw Alan open his mouth to protest, but she beat him to the punch. "I'm a talk-show host, not a life host."

He said the one thing that was guaranteed to make her capitulate. "This could boost ratings. Sweeps are coming up, and we need a gimmick."

She groaned and rolled her eyes. Glancing toward MacKenzie, she saw no help in that quarter.

"Please don't make me do this, Alan." But even as she made the entreaty, the sinking sensation that her fate had already been sealed overtook her.

Alan looked utterly confused at her reluctance. "What's the matter? I thought you'd be thrilled to live with a good-looking man."

She'd just assumed that he'd been around during her working hours. This was even worse than she thought. "I have to live with him?"

Alan nodded. The details had already been worked out with the man who had returned with MacKenzie. "For a couple of weeks."

"A couple of weeks?" she echoed incredulously. My God, that was an eternity. She tried to suppress a wave of annoyance. One would think that after all this time, she wouldn't have to resort to gimmicks to hang on to her audience.

"Couldn't I just live with a Bengal tiger for a couple of weeks instead? Damn it, Alan, it's an invasion of privacy, it's living with an albatross around my neck, it's—"

Alan looked at her innocently as he said the magic words. "It's sweeps month."

She sighed, knowing that he was right, that at the last staff meeting, she'd found that they didn't have a gimmick in place for the occasion that governed the lives of everyone in television. During sweeps month everyone tried to outdo the other for the tiniest percentage point. Resignation did not feel good.

She looked at MacKenzie. "Do I at least get to choose which one?"

She couldn't read MacKenzie's expression as the latter said, "The audience already chose for you."

"Of course they did." Dakota was afraid to ask. Maybe because she already knew the answer. It was Ian. Why else would Alan care if she was building "a rapport" or not? Still, she heard herself asking, "And which one did they pick?"

"They picked Ian." MacKenzie told her.

A spark of hope rose to the surface of the quicksand in which she found herself standing. "He's never going to go for this."

MacKenzie wasn't fazed. "Randy was very excited about the idea. A little put off that he wasn't the one the audience wanted, but he still thinks this is a great idea."

It didn't matter what the other man thought of the idea. He wasn't the one who would endure being a body-guard to a woman whose body didn't need guarding.

"Ian is not going to go for this," Dakota repeated. She might not know him all that well, but she recognized stubbornness when she saw it.

Alan began again, more insistently this time. "But if he does—"

Never happen, she thought happily.

She loved her show, didn't mind doing strange stunts, but they only lasted for a few hours at the most. This threatened to take out a large chunk of her life, and she didn't want to volunteer it. The last thing she wanted was to have a good-looking man hovering over her as if she was some dolt incapable of tying her own shoes or crossing the street without getting hit by a car.

"Then I'm on board," she told him with the casual assurance of someone who felt that could never happen.

Alan grinned. "Then you'd better prepare your boarding pass."

The sinking feeling was back, larger than before. "Why?"

Alan beamed, well pleased with himself. "Because I offered to hook them up with someone who could do a commercial for their firm. I'm having the station un-derwrite the costs."

It didn't get any better than that. She could see how the men, especially Randy, would have a difficult time turning that down.

So she was going to have a roommate for the next two weeks. "You play dirty."

Alan made his way to the door, then stopped to look at her before leaving. "Never said I didn't."

"No."

The single word was a cross between some unintelligible guttural sound and a bear growling. All the more intimidating because it had come out of Ian's barely moving lips.

Randy had pounced on his friend with the news the moment he'd walked into the office. He'd been behind Ian by five minutes and was still hearing the promises ringing in his ears.

The two men now stood facing each other on opposite sides of the small reception desk. Wanda, Randy's younger sister who manned the desk when she wasn't taking classes at NYU, had wisely chosen to retreat from the field until the battle was over.

"Russell, just think about the possibilities—" Randy begged.

"No," Ian repeated more firmly. "Look, I did the show because you asked me to, even though I didn't think we needed it. I am not going to play nursemaid to some celebrity as a publicity stunt."

For the life of him, Randy couldn't see what the big

deal was. Or the difference—other than a slew of benefits and a stack of money. "It's not a stunt, Russell, and why should this be any different from anything you do as a regular bodyguard?"

As far as he was concerned, there was a world of difference. "Because in all the other cases, there was a real threat, a possible danger. We were keeping someone safe and out of harm's way. This is just a game, a lark dreamed up by some publicity guy with nothing to do—"

"That's what he does do," Randy pointed out. "Come up with gimmicks to help the show. In this case, it's helping us as well."

"I don't need that kind of help," Ian insisted. He shoved his hands into his pockets. He never should have said yes to Taylor in the first place. They were doing well enough without this. "It's a game," he repeated. "And I'm no good with nothing to do."

Randy threw up his hands, clearly annoyed with his partner's stubbornness.

"Then pretend she has a stalker. Pretend you're keeping her safe. Damn it, Russell, have a little imagination. The bodyguard business is about keeping our clients safe from overzealous fans and the invading photographers. From what I saw of that audience today, Dakota Delany's got a hell of a lot of fans." He paused, then added more quietly, "John Lennon was killed by a fan."

Okay, so maybe Taylor had a point. That still didn't

mean he had to be the one to do this. There was something about being in that woman's company that told him he shouldn't be. But it wasn't something he was about to share with Taylor, who felt that everything with supple hips bore exploring.

"Why can't you do it?"

Randy raised his wide shoulders and let them drop in an almost helpless movement. "Because they want you. The producer said you and Dakota had chemistry."

Ian swung around and looked at him incredulously. "We had what?"

"Chemistry," Randy enunciated. "That's when two people—"

Ian glared at him. "I know what chemistry is. And we—she and I—don't have it."

Ian found the smirk on Randy's face particularly irritating.

"I don't know about that," Randy murmured under his breath.

Eyes narrowing, Ian got into his face. "What's that supposed to mean?"

Randy raised his hands to ward off his partner's words. "Hey, stay focused. We're arguing about you doing this. I don't want this to escalate into some kind of a full-out war between us." He tried again, his voice softening. "I was right about this, Ian. On the way over here I got three calls on my cell phone alone. Wanda's been fielding calls. Business is already picking up."

The calls would have come one way or another. "We're heading into the award season in a couple of months," Ian pointed out.

"I don't want just seasonal work, do you?"

Ian frowned. No, he didn't want just seasonal work. He wanted to be kept busy all year round. Maybe then the heartache of not being around his son, of not being able to watch Scottie grow up, wouldn't keep eating away at him the way that it was.

A sense of resignation slipped in. So he'd do this. What would it hurt? He pinned Randy with a look. "If I do this, it's going to be my way."

Randy raised both hands up in innocent surrender. As if, Ian thought jadedly. "Absolutely."

"I'm going to approach this seriously," Ian qualified, "as if this Delany woman actually needed a professional bodyguard to protect her."

"Wouldn't have it any other way," Randy agreed. "Oh, one more thing. The studio wants you to live at her apartment for the duration of the assignment."

He'd only done that twice before and hadn't liked it either time. He definitely didn't like giving up his freedom, especially not when there was nothing more than a whim involved. "Taylor—"

"They're paying us double our usual fee to do it, plus free publicity." Randy held up his hand and continued more quickly, "Plus the producer's going to have the studio underwriting a commercial for the firm."

"Just to have us do this?"

"It's called sweetening the pot," Randy said. "I told them that you'd be reluctant."

Ian laughed shortly. "That's the first time I've ever heard you understate something."

"Then you'll do it?"

Ian parked himself on the edge of the desk. Something in his gut told him he was going to regret this, but for the good of the company, he was going to have to take this bullet.

"If I don't, you'll probably nag me to death." He might as well be prepared. "When do I start?"

Randy's eyes avoided his. "Tomorrow morning."

"Tomorrow?" As if on cue, the phone rang. Ian nodded toward the instrument. "What about business?"

Randy placed his hand on the receiver but didn't pick up yet. "If it gets too much for me to handle, I can call in some favors. I know a couple of guys on the job who wouldn't mind moonlighting."

A lot of policemen made extra money in either security work or acting as temporary bodyguards. Right now he was willing to change places with any of them. "Maybe one of them wouldn't mind taking my assignment."

Randy shook his head. "Hey, what's the problem? From where I was sitting, that was one mighty fine lady."

Maybe that *was* the problem. "I'm not interested in 'mighty fine' ladies."

Randy shut his eyes as if searching for strength. The phone continued ringing. "You were divorced, Ian, you weren't neutered. There are times I really do despair about you." With a heartfelt sigh, he picked up the telephone receiver. "Bodyguard, Inc. How can I help you?"

Ian tuned him out as he went to the door. If this was going to happen tomorrow, he needed to go home to pack.

And to seriously rethink the career choice that had brought him to this junction. Ian headed toward the elevator. Paperwork was beginning not to sound so bad.

She was not an early riser.

Early to Dakota meant that the world was already well bathed in sunlight, people were brewing coffee and, like as not, on their way to whatever life had to offer them that day. Dawn was something she customarily visited from the other side of the night.

Which was what made her impromptu trip upstate so unexpected, most of all to her. It was definitely not a habit she felt the least bit inclined to acquire.

She was not one of those people who bounced out of bed unless, like that one time back home, there was an earthquake demanding her attention. So when she heard first the doorbell, then a hard, firm knock on the front door of her thirtieth-floor penthouse apartment, she pretty much thought she was dreaming.

As the knocking persisted, growing louder, the dream turned into a nightmare and then vanished altogether, leaving her brain enshrouded in a fog thick enough to sock in any airport.

The knocking turned into banging, the sound vibrating in her head.

More than half-asleep, she tumbled out of bed, the comforter pooling behind her on the floor like an afterthought. She made one futile attempt at shoving her feet into slippers, had a fifty-percent success rate and half stumbled, half dragged herself to the front door. Anything to stop the awful banging.

She felt around on the wall in the general vicinity of the light switch. After finding it, she threw it on and blinked as the light blinded her.

"What!" she demanded angrily as she yanked open the door.

Ian stood on the other side of the door, magnificent in his anger and obvious disapproval. Marching into the apartment, he firmly shut the door behind him. The sound resonated in her chest. If looks could kill, she had a feeling she would have found herself skewered on a spit, about to become a large piece of charcoal.

"Are you crazy?" he demanded. The woman hadn't even bothered to ask who it was. He could have been some serial killer, looking to gain access to her apartment. Or, at the very least, he could have been a stalker. Maybe this woman *did* need someone in her life to keep her safe. Apparently she didn't have the brains of a pair of size-six shoes.

Sucking in air, Dakota dragged a hand through her hair. It fell haphazardly about her face. Clarity to her brain still refused to surface.

"I must be," she agreed vaguely. "I'm having a conversation in my dream. Or maybe it's a nightmare.

There's some man standing in my foyer, yelling at me." She squinted. "Wait, he looks just like that man who was on my show yesterday."

Ian glared at her as if she was babbling in some foreign tongue. Only slowly did he become aware of the fact that the woman was wearing some football jersey that had seen a dozen or so too many cycles in the washing machine and had worn to the thickness of overused gauze. In addition, it apparently had shrunk rather badly. With the light shining behind her, he could see the complete outline of her body, covered by the thin fabric.

Muscles he wasn't aware of having tightened all throughout his body.

Ian fixed his glare on the top of her tousled hair. That way, he felt a hell of a lot less unsettled. "You don't open the door like that."

"Only way I know how to open it." She blinked several times, trying to get a lock on the situation. "Did you come here to argue?"

"I came here to be your bodyguard," he reminded her tersely.

It took her a moment to process. She squinted at him again. "Doesn't that mean I'm supposed to be the one in charge?"

Had she been completely conscious and in possession of all her faculties, she would have seen that the expression on his face was foreboding. "Within limits."

"How about games?"

He couldn't begin to follow her. "What?"

She took a deep breath before continuing. "Am I in charge of games?"

That made less than no sense to him. He sniffed the air around her. No, she wasn't drunk or getting over the effects of being in that condition. "Yes, sure, games." Maybe the woman was just plain crazy, he decided.

"Fine," she exhaled the word. "We're playing Simon Says. Simon says go back to bed. 'Night."

And as he watched, Dakota turned on her heel and stumbled out of the room. It was only then that he realized she was wearing just one slipper.

And that in all likelihood he had been celibate much too long.

Chapter Six

Usually Dakota could go back to sleep no matter what. Even during the earthquake episode, once her bed had stopped shuddering like a wet dog coming out of the river, she was able to fall asleep again.

But having some brooding, good-looking man she hardly knew hovering around her apartment was different. All she managed to achieve was a half sleep filled with dreams of him that seemed very, very real while she was having them.

She gave up a half hour later. After getting out of bed, she got dressed before venturing from her bedroom. The rest of the apartment was very quiet. There was no sound, no evidence that there was someone else here.

Maybe she'd somehow dreamed up the whole thing.

On her way to the kitchen and some life-affirming coffee, she peeked into the room she'd converted into her office then stopped dead.

Ian perused the bookcase in the room that his pseudo client obviously used as an office. A desk and two bookcases filled the sunny room. Photographs were hung on every available wall space. Photographs of Dakota with celebrities she'd had on the show.

On her desk were more private photographs. One of a man he vaguely recognized and a smiling woman who looked like an older version of Dakota. Those had to be her parents. There was one of her and the man who'd secretly been his boyhood hero: Waylon Montgomery. Ian had been eleven when he'd arrived at the conclusion that no man was a hero. But until then, the man who played Savage Ben's owner had been it for him. Another photograph was of her and a man he assumed was her brother.

Two frames stood empty, and this aroused his curiosity. He was just about to examine them when he heard her voice and turned around.

"You weren't a dream," she said. He was there, his back to the door. For a man who stood approximately six feet tall, he still somehow managed to look larger than life.

She looked a great deal more presentable. The football jersey had been replaced by a navy miniskirt with white accents and a navy sweater that showed off her assets. Still, the fact that she was no longer wearing a gauzelike jersey allowed him to look somewhere other than just her eyes.

"Nobody's ever accused me of being that," he commented, mildly amused. He nodded at the frame he was holding. "What's with the empty frames?"

There'd been two photographs, one of John alone and one taken of the two of them at the last fund-raiser they'd attended. Both photographs had met a quick demise when she'd discovered just how closely John liked working with his patients after they'd recovered. "I didn't like the pictures that were there anymore."

Part of his job was to read people, and she was almost transparent. "Boyfriend?" he guessed.

She shrugged a tad too carelessly in his estimation, confirming his suspicions as she walked into the room. "Something like that."

He set the frame back down in its space. "Oh."

On the defensive, Dakota raised her eyes to his. "What, 'oh'?"

Ian looked at her for a long moment. "You were serious about him."

Self-preservation had her wanting to deny it, but there was no point in lying. Ian's X-ray vision would probably alert him to it anyway.

"More than he was about me, apparently." She went on the offensive. "Is this what a bodyguard does, ask questions he shouldn't? I thought you were the strong, silent type."

As far as he was concerned, he didn't have a type. He just did his job to the best of his ability. "Just trying to get the lay of the land."

With effort, she forced herself to stop being defensive. John was history, and as part of hers, she was going to have to deal with it. For now she had something else to deal with, this man in her apartment. "You're taking this whole thing seriously, aren't you?"

He took everything seriously, but saying so would probably start her off on some tangent, so he merely said, "The kind of money your studio is paying for this, there's no other way to take it but seriously."

"You could try having fun with this."

Spoken like someone who'd been pampered all her life, he thought. "I'm not being paid to have fun." Ian looked at her intently. "Being a bodyguard is very serious business."

His eyes had turned a very interesting shade of gray, she thought. Almost like dusk settling in over the horizon. Just what she needed getting in her way, a dour man. He had to lighten up. "I don't have a stalker," she asserted.

Ian's expression never changed. "That you know of."

"Thanks for that cheerful thought."

"That's the only effective way for a bodyguard to operate. As if each client had someone out there who could harm them at any given moment. I'm supposed to keep you safe."

Dakota suddenly grinned at him and was determined

to have a little fun. Sidling up to Ian, she left enough room between their bodies for a flea to get through. A flea that had successfully completed a crash diet. "And what's to keep you safe?"

She was trying to shake him up. But knowing didn't prevent the flare of heat from igniting inside of him. The earlier image of her body, almost completely visible and highly inviting, flashed across his mind. Ian banked down it and his reaction.

"I'm packing a gun," he informed her evenly, answering her question.

Releasing the breath she was holding, Dakota laughed as she stepped back. "That'll do it."

Moving out of the room, she nearly tripped over the suitcase she hadn't noticed before. Off balance, she had no time to steady herself. In a heartbeat, strong hands were on either side of her shoulders, keeping her body from ignobly meeting the rug.

As she looked up at him, she found that she had somehow managed to lose the air from her lungs. It took her a second to recover and covertly attempt to draw in air.

She hoped she could cover the moment with a smile. "You *do* take this protecting thing very seriously, don't you?"

He released her, aware that he'd held her a beat too long and that the sensation of having her so close was more pleasant than it should have been. He was going to have to watch that, he told himself.

"The studio opted for the whole package," he reminded her.

And what a package it was, she caught herself thinking. Trying to get her bearings, she looked down at the culprit that had caused her to trip. She didn't believe in clutter. Consequently she knew where everything was within her apartment and could easily maneuver around it in the dark. This hadn't been there earlier.

"A suitcase?"

He nodded as he pushed it to the side with his foot. "For my clothes."

It took a second for his words to sink in. "You agreed to *stay* here?" She would have bet anything he would have vetoed that part of it.

"I do for the more intense assignments."

She could feel the space around her shrinking by the second. "And I'm an intense assignment?"

He shrugged, obviously far less troubled by his choice of words than she was. "Like I said, the studio wanted the whole package."

She sighed, shaking her head. She and Alan Curtis were going to have a very long talk when she came in today. Saying yes to the producer's proposal didn't mean she'd given him carte blanche with her life.

But for now she was going to have to make the best of it. Her father had taught her that making the best of it was how one survived. "C'mon, I'll show you to your room."

Ian made no move to pick up his suitcase and follow

her. "I thought this would do." He nodded toward the sofa. "I could sack out there."

"This is my office." It was going to be hard enough to share her apartment with him. She wasn't about to share her work space as well. "I have a spare bedroom." Her tone made things final.

With another half shrug, Ian picked up his suitcase. "You're the boss."

She smiled as she led the way out. "I think I could get used to the sound of that."

He realized he was staring at her hips again and drew his eyes up to look at the back of her head. A second later he replayed her comment. He could easily see her running off with that as some kind of promise. "Within reason."

Turning toward the small corridor, she glanced over her shoulder at him. "Meaning?"

His lips never curved. "Meaning that if you wanted to run naked into a crowd of people, I'd have to override you."

Turning just before reaching the bedroom, she took his words as a direct challenge. "If I wanted to be naked, what right do you have to stop me?"

"I'm being paid to use my judgment about how to keep you safe. Running naked into the crowd somehow strikes me as not really keeping you safe—for long."

She laughed lightly, conceding the point. And then the skin along her neck turned to goose bumps. About to open the door, she realized that she hadn't been in this room since John had moved out. She should have realized something was not quite right with the arrangement when he'd told her he wanted a room of his own. At the time, she'd just thought he needed work space. She hadn't realized that they had different definitions for the word.

She'd had Eva, the woman who came in once a month to clean, air the bedroom out so that not even a telltale scent of his cologne was left in the room.

But the woman had forgotten to vacuum out the memories, she thought.

"I guess I'll just have to keep my clothes on," he murmured.

Everything within the room was brand-new. The curtains, the bedspread, everything that carried with it even the slightest memory was gone.

She felt oddly liberated as she stood now, looking in.

Ian walked to the closet and opened the sliding mirrored door to deposit his suitcase. As he did so, he noticed that there was a blue shirt hanging at the far left of the closet, all the way against one wall.

He pulled it out and held it up. "Or throw this on."

She had once thrown on that shirt, she recalled. As a joke. John had been fussing about his clothing, telling her that she was wrinkling his jacket when she'd laughingly pushed him back on the bed. To tease him, she'd donned one of his shirts over some very fancy underwear. He'd been more concerned about the condition of his custom-made shirt than he had about what was underneath it at the time.

She should have realized they were worlds apart then.

Had he left the shirt here on purpose, in hopes of haunting her, of making her call him in order to tell him that she hadn't meant to throw him out?

If he had, he'd certainly misjudged her.

Pulling the blue garment off its hanger, she bunched the shirt into a ball and threw it into the wastepaper basket. She tossed her head, sending her long, blond hair flying over her shoulder.

"Not if it was the last garment on earth and the world was slipping into another Ice Age."

Ian heard something beyond the words. "Hurt you that badly, did he?"

It wasn't hurt, not after the initial ten minutes. "No, just made me realize what an idiot I was for settling."

He cocked his head slightly to the side, as if trying to make sense out of what she was saying. "Settling?"

For reasons she couldn't fathom, it made her impatient to explain.

"I wanted what my parents had. What they *have*," she corrected. Anyone in the room with her parents could easily see the two still loved each other as much now as they had the day they got married. "Happiness. I thought that maybe John could give it to me. I got fooled by the trappings and ignored the man beneath." She stopped abruptly and looked at him accusingly. "Do we have to have this conversation?"

"No." There was passion there when she spoke, he thought. In her eyes. They grew brighter, lighter if that was possible. As it was, it looked as if God had taken His cue for how the sky should look from her eyes.

She had to change the subject. It made her no happier to think about having to share the next two weeks—and her apartment—with a stranger who had caught her audience's fancy. A stranger who intended to shadow her every move. She wondered if the ratings were worth it.

"What do you need, in order to settle in?" she asked, doing her best not to sound as if she was talking about an upcoming execution.

His suitcase inside the closet, he slid the door closed again, then looked at her. "I'm 'in,'" he informed her simply.

She laughed and shook her head. When John had moved in, he had needed seven trips to bring in all his belongings. She was a firm believer in quality. With him, it had been quantity. Lots and lots of quantity. Her huge apartment had been crowded.

It appeared that Ian Russell was even more of a minimalist than she was. "Don't require much, do you?"

His eyes met hers again. "Just cooperation."

She banked down the shiver that found its way up and down her spine. "Ah, well, that's going to be the hard part, I suspect." She turned and walked out of the room.

He was right behind her. "It can be as easy or as hard as you make it."

She stopped and turned to look at him. "In other words, it's all up to me."

He spread his hands. "In any words, it's all up to you."

She wasn't buying that for one moment. This was not an easygoing man, this was a man who was accustomed to being obeyed.

"As long as I do what you tell me."

He smiled just then and she was struck by the way his face seemed to change and soften. "Those are the words," he agreed.

Her breath had lodged in her lungs again. What the hell was wrong with her this morning? she upbraided herself. "You should do that more often."

A slight look of confusion told her that he didn't follow her reference. "Do what?"

She subdued the urge to trace his smile with her fingertips. Coffee, she told herself, she needed coffee. "Smile."

He looked at her steadily. "I wasn't aware that I was."

She'd embarrassed him and felt a salvo of triumph shooting through her veins. A sense of glee burrowed through her. Maybe she could somehow manage to have fun with this assignment even with an albatross around her neck. "You were and it makes you look human."

"Human costs extra," he told her, his smile disappearing as if it had never existed.

"I'll talk to the studio," she promised. Turning on her heel, she continued heading toward the kitchen. "So, you're just going to follow me around all day?"

"That's the plan."

A thought suddenly occurred to her. How far was he

thinking of taking this? "You're not going to sit on the stage with me, are you?"

Sitting under those hot lights with powder on his face was an experience he had no intentions of duplicating. "No."

She pretended to look distressed. "But I might be attacked by a falling sandbag or—"

"Some things we leave to chance. But very little," he said before she could take the comment and run. Dakota opened her mouth to say something, but his cell phone began to ring.

"Looks like you're wanted," she said. She started to turn down the hallway. She paused just long enough to wink at him. "Oh, by the way, I'll be in the kitchen if you're wondering."

With a slightly less than curt nod, he turned his attention toward his cell phone. Had Randy changed his mind about being able to handle the home front single-handedly? If the phones were going to ring off the hook the way his partner hoped, they would have their hands full of real assignments instead of this make-believe one.

Sincerely hoping he was right, Ian flipped open his phone.

"Russell." The next moment, he heard a voice in his ear that was all too familiar to him. Ian curbed his quick flash of impatience. "Yes, hello Alexis. Wait, slow down. What?"

The woman on the other end had been his first case only days after he and Randy set up their firm. She'd come to them, claiming that a stalker was after her. He'd recognized her as someone he'd questioned in connection with a crime while he was still a homicide detective. Very quickly it became apparent to him that the whole story about a stalker had been a ruse. As politely as he could, he'd taken himself off her case. Periodically she called back, still claiming that someone was after her.

He now listened as Alexis went through a hysterical litany. When she showed no signs of letting up, he finally broke in.

"Did you try the other two firms I gave you?" Sending her to the police was no use. They'd already proven that her stories were fabrications. "Well, you have to give them time, Alexis. I'm sure that one of them—no, I'm afraid I'm busy right now," he told her firmly as she began to plead. "It's a new assignment. I'm going to be busy for at least the next two months. Possibly longer. Right. Well, I can't stop you from calling in two months, but I really recommend that you go to one of the other firms. They have more manpower. Right. Yeah, sorry. Bye," he said quickly before she could get a second wind, then quickly flipped his phone closed again.

He pushed Off before slipping it back into his pocket.

As he began to turn the corner, he walked right into Dakota. His brows narrowed. She'd obviously heard every word. "I thought you said you were on your way to the kitchen."

"I was," she told him innocently, "but that sounded

just too tempting to pass up. Yes, eavesdropping, I know." She beat him to the accusation. "Sorry, occupational hazard." She grinned at him. "But then, you know all about that, I imagine." Since he'd all but grilled her, she thought turnabout was only fair. She cocked her head. "Old girlfriend?"

He blew out a breath. Alexis had probably seen him on the talk show, and that had been enough to get her going again. "Old client."

"'Old' as in former," she asked, "or as in having so many candles to blow out on her cake, the paramedic is on standby?"

"The first." The woman asked way too many questions, he thought.

He glared at her, but she didn't let that stop her. Her curiosity had taken wing. "What happened? Your company drop her?"

What happened was that he had quickly gotten wise to what was going on. He kept it simple. "She didn't need a bodyguard. She wanted a warm body."

As he watched, a grin bloomed on her lips. It had a captivating quality even as it annoyed him. "Yours, I take it."

He shrugged it off. "It's nothing personal," he maintained. "Women fall in love with their doctors, with the fireman who rescues them—"

"With the bodyguard who's a hunk," she interjected easily.

He looked at her sharply. The whole thing obviously amused her. "It's not funny."

"What?" she asked innocently. "Being a hunk? Is that serious with you, too?"

"I am not a—" He caught himself before his temper had a chance to take hold. "Do you plan to be this antagonistic the whole two weeks?"

"Antagonistic?" she echoed, her hand delicately placed on her chest. "I thought I was being friendly." And then she winked at him. "Believe me, you'll know when I'm antagonistic. According to my father, my eyes start to shoot thunderbolts and my skin gets this really bright shade of red."

Ian snorted. "Thanks for the warning."

She walked into the kitchen, went straight to the wall phone and picked up the receiver. Her stomach rumbled a protest. "Want some breakfast?" she asked as she pulled the number of a restaurant off the refrigerator.

He stared at her in disbelief. "Are you ordering takeout?"

Her finger poised over the keypad, she glanced at him. "Sure."

He strode past her to the refrigerator. "What do you have in your refrigerator?"

She thought a moment. "Last I checked, a lightbulb and some shelves."

He opened it and looked for himself. She was right. Empty. Not even what he'd come to expect. "No bottled water?" he scoffed.

She'd never picked up the habit of carrying around overpriced water that came from heaven only knew where. "I like New York water," she informed him. "It's got character." She watched as he closed the refrigerator and walked toward the front door. "Have I scared you off already?"

He paused only long enough to issue instructions. "Stay here and have some coffee." He nodded at the coffeemaker she must have preprogrammed the night before. "I'm going to the grocery store."

Sliding off the stool, she accompanied him to the door. "Sure I'll be safe?"

He ignored her sarcastic tone. Thirteen days after today, he told himself. Just thirteen more days. "Just don't throw open your door without asking who it is again."

He saw her salute, then suddenly disappear from the doorway. But as he turned away he heard her call after him. "Wait."

Now what? Stifling impatience, he turned from the elevator. "What?"

"Here." Striding toward him, her door hanging open in the background, she placed the spare key that had once belonged to John in the palm of his hand, then closed his fingers around it. She was very aware that his fingers felt strong, manly, and that she couldn't help wondering if they'd be that strong gliding along her body. "This way we won't have to play twenty questions through the door and you won't have to lecture me again." She looked at him significantly. "The first lecture's okay. The second one I might bite."

He nodded, pocketing the key. "I'll try to remember that," he told her as he went to the elevator.

"You do that, Ian," she murmured under her breath just before returning to her apartment. "You be sure to do that."

Chapter Seven

Ian returned less than half an hour later, carrying two large grocery bags filled to the brim with everything he needed to make breakfast. Rather than use the key she'd given him, he rang the doorbell.

"Who is it?"

He allowed himself a small grin of triumph. At least she was learning. "It's Ian."

"Ian who?" came the melodious question through the door.

"Russell," he replied evenly. Holding the bags was awkward to say the least. He shifted them for a better hold.

"How do I know you're who you say you are?"

Okay, no triumph, he thought. She was being deliberately difficult. "Look through the peephole," he growled.

He heard some movement going on behind the door. The next moment she opened it to admit him. "Never can be too careful," she told him innocently. Dakota eyed the bags as he shouldered his way in past her. "Boy, what have you got there?"

"Breakfast," he informed her tersely.

She'd changed, he noticed as he carried the bags into the kitchen. But she obviously wasn't in work attire. Despite the weather, she was wearing shorts and an old sweatshirt. From her body language, he gathered that he'd caught her on the way out. Had he come in five minutes later, he had no doubt that he would have missed her.

Ian rested the bags on the counter and looked at her. "Where are you going?"

"Out jogging." She started to turn on her heel. "Don't worry, I'll be back soon."

"Hold it." Picking up the bags again, he shoved both into the refrigerator and turned around. The look on his face told her he wasn't fooling around. "It'll take me three minutes to get ready."

Anxious to get going, to work off some of this tension that having him here created, she shifted from foot to foot. "Ready for what?"

He said what she didn't want to hear. "I'm going with you."

Dakota frowned. This was carrying pretense a bit

far. After all, it wasn't as if she actually *needed* a body-guard. The people she ran into were all friendly.

"You don't have to," she told him. "I've been jogging every morning, rain or shine, since I was fifteen years old."

"Wait," he ordered sternly as he ducked back into the guest room.

She had no idea why she was listening to him. After all, she had free will, didn't she? Even so, she approached his door rather than the one that led to the outside.

"I've got half a mind to leave." She raised her voice in order to be heard through the closed door.

"That's exactly what you have," he agreed. "Half a mind."

Ian threw open the door. Along with jogging shoes, he wore sweatpants and an old sweatshirt that might have fit him once, but was now a size too small and strained against his muscles.

She didn't think it was humanly possible to change clothes so quickly. Too bad he couldn't change his manners that fast.

"What's that supposed to mean?" she asked as she followed him to the front door.

Securing the door after she walked out, he then led the way to the elevator. "Where do you jog?" he asked.

Since her penthouse was located only a block away from Central Park, she thought the answer was rather obvious. "Around the park."

Over the years, because of the efforts of the police

force, Central Park had once more become a safe place for people to go. Up to a degree.

"Alone?"

She pretended to check her pockets for any small creatures. "Nope, no hitchhikers here." She looked at him as she walked into the elevator car that had just arrived. "Yes, alone." When he had first moved in with her, she'd tried to convince John to jog with her, but he hadn't been into any kind of sport that required wearing sneakers.

"Don't you realize that you risk getting kidnapped?" he demanded. "There are places along the park where—"

She didn't like his tone. He had no right to think he was in charge of her even if she'd hired him to be her bodyguard, which she hadn't. She raised her hand, stopping him before he could get any further.

"You don't have to tell me, my ex-fiancé told me all about it." The express elevator made it down to the first floor before she could finish her thought. The doors opened and she immediately was on her way. "I can't live life like that, always afraid."

He caught up to her before they exited the building. "Not afraid," he chided, "just sensible." Longing to stretch his legs, he forced himself to keep abreast of her as he tried to make her see the light. "You keep Band-Aids in your medicine cabinet, don't you?"

"Yes." She sent him a look that was more annoyed than she realized. Ever since she was a little girl, she'd hated having people tell her what to do. "What does that have to do with anything?"

"Judging by the way you talk, you're not always worried about getting cuts, are you?"

As they approached the park, she began to pour it on. She noted Ian kept up without trying. "No."

"Then why the Band-Aids? To be prepared, right?" The light was with them, and they ran across the street, entering the urban anomaly. "In case you need one. Sensible."

She blew out a breath. It was going to be a long five miles. "If you say so."

Forty-five minutes later, they were back in her apartment. Dakota did her best not to let him see just how much she'd pushed to keep up. She could swear she felt every bone in her body and they were all protesting. As they'd talked—or he'd lectured and she'd retorted— Ian had consciously or unconsciously set the pace. It was faster than her usual pace, but she was damned if she was going to ask him to slow down or shorten his stride.

She'd pushed harder this morning than she could ever remember pushing. She felt exhaustion, mingled with the special brand of euphoria that set in whenever a runner hit that magical zone where all things came together, made sense and created a sense of well-being.

Upon their return, Ian closed the door behind them.

He didn't even look winded, the rat. He did look sweaty, which was sexy on him.

Then again, blueberry muffins would have looked sexy on him, she decided.

"Why don't you shower?" he suggested, taking the towel she'd handed him. He could smell her perspiration on it. Something small, anonymous and disconcerting tightened in his gut. "I'll get breakfast going."

The thought of cleanliness and distance appealed to her. She didn't argue.

Fifteen minutes later she was looking down at French toast and an arrangement of small turkey sausages surrounding a single fried egg, over easy. It was as if he'd entered her head.

She looked at him warily. "How did you know?"

"Research." Walking out of the kitchen, he went to take his own shower. Dakota noted that there were no pans or utensils in the sink. They were drying on the rack. The man was in a class by himself.

That still didn't change the fact that having him underfoot and wedged obtrusively into her life was going to be a problem.

She drove to work with Ian in the passenger seat. She was surprised that he relinquished control this way without a word.

But the words came soon enough. And they centered around the hazards of jogging by herself and of opening the door without first checking to see who was standing on the other side. Then he got on to the topic of her having a security system installed.

He was taking all this much too seriously, she thought. She spared him a look at a red light. "You're just pretending to be my bodyguard, remember?"

"The risks you're taking aren't pretend. You're inviting trouble."

Dakota bit her tongue as she glanced at him. She already had, she thought. And the invitation was not by choice. There was no way she was going to be able to survive two weeks of this.

Parking the car in her spot in the underground garage, she went to the elevator and punched the up button, fleetingly debating taking the stairs. She wanted to see the producer posthaste.

As Ian began to follow her out of the elevator, she looked over her shoulder at him and ordered, "Stay."

"I'm a bodyguard, not a dog," he told her. "Maybe you should look into the difference."

"I already know the difference," she told him. "Dogs obey. Look, I have something private to discuss with Alan. You have to wait in the hall. If Alan turns out to secretly be a Ninja warrior, I promise I'll call for you."

She left him scowling in the hallway as she marched into Alan Curtis's outer office. Felicity, Alan's secretary, looked surprised to see her. "He's on the phone—"

"He's got two ears," she answered tersely.

She swung open the door to Alan's inner office. Alan

was indeed on the phone, but this didn't stop her. Without any greeting or preamble, Dakota held up her index finger and declared, "One week."

"Hold on a sec," Alan said to the person on the other end of the line. He pressed the hold button, then looked at the star of his station's best daytime program.

"Two," he countered.

He wasn't about to give an inch, she thought. And as producer, Alan did have final say. Feeling trapped, she demanded, "Why two?"

He laid the receiver on his shoulder, giving her his attention. "Because it takes almost two weeks for a routine to set in."

Dakota shook her head. "Trust me, there's no routine setting in."

Affable, known as a pussycat among those he worked with, Alan Curtis was no one's pushover. And he was savvy when it came to the viewing public.

Alan remained firm. "Two weeks."

Dakota was never one of those personalities who threw tantrums to get what she wanted. She sighed heavily, accepting defeat for the good of the show. Certainly not her own good. "Okay, but you pay for the defense lawyer if I kill him."

Alan settled back in his chair again and nodded solemnly. "Already got one on retainer. James Patrick. Good man."

She stopped in the doorway, giving him a disparaging look. "More than I can say about you, Alan."

"Sweeps," Alan said in reply just before he pressed the hold button again and got back to his phone call.

The moment she was in the outer office, MacKenzie was on her, her eyes eager for details. She dropped her voice in order to avoid being heard by either Felicity or the man she'd passed standing in the hallway. "So, how's the new man in your life working out?"

"He's not the new man in my life and he's not working out."

MacKenzie sighed deeply as she looked over her shoulder out into the hall. "He's too beautiful not to work out."

Dakota knew more than anyone that good looks meant nothing. It was what was underneath that counted and Ian Russell's "underneath" was a heavy dose of "annoying."

"Fine, you live with a bodyguard for two weeks."

"It's not my show." MacKenzie's expression became a shade more serious. "C'mon, Dakota, it's not so bad."

A lot she knew, Dakota thought. "Yes, it is. Even if he kept his mouth shut—which he didn't—it's still unsettling having this huge, muscular shadow hovering around wherever I go." She wasn't getting the response she wanted out of MacKenzie. "Zee, the man jogged with me."

MacKenzie clutched her chest. "The nerve of the man. He should be flogged." And then she laughed. "So he jogged with you, so what? It's nice to have a jogging partner. Remember, you tried to get me to jog with you. And John."

Just what she needed, a friend with a good memory. "Neither one of you would have lectured about the dangers of someone like me jogging alone."

"He has a point."

Dakota closed her eyes, sighing. This wasn't working out right. "Don't you start, too." She looked into the hall. He was still standing there like some kind of stone statue. A statue she had no doubt would suddenly launch into action at the first sign of some unauthorized person approaching her. "I'm surprised he doesn't tell me not to take candy from strangers."

"Hey, don't work yourself up. He can guard my body anyday."

"I'll make you a present of him when this is over." Sooner, if she could.

But MacKenzie was right, Dakota thought. It wasn't the other woman's show, it was hers, which meant that sometimes she had to do what she didn't want to do. This was right up there with getting hit in the face with custard pies.

Except that she liked custard.

She looked at MacKenzie. "By the way, how did it go with Randy?"

MacKenzie shrugged carelessly. "It went. He has a girlfriend."

She felt a prick of disappointment for her friend. She knew that MacKenzie, unlike her, was ripe for a relationship and wanted all the trimmings. "I'm sorry."

Another shrug followed on the heels of the first. "Don't be. Story of my life." She hooked her arm through Dakota's. "C'mon, let's get you into makeup." Walking out, she grinned at Ian. "You can watch, handsome."

There was no doubt in Dakota's mind that he would.

Her audience went wild when she told them about the experiment. Because she knew they expected it, she played the entire thing up, telling them that Ian had moved into her guest bedroom for the next two weeks. She got exactly the response she'd anticipated. Oohs and aahs of envy resounded throughout the studio as well as catcalls. The audience was enjoying this.

Dakota glanced toward the wings and saw that her faithful, if pseudo, bodyguard was indeed standing there, observing. Any woman would feel safe with him on the job, she couldn't help thinking. Any woman but her. She already felt safe. What she felt right now was vaguely claustrophobic.

And then, as she looked at his stoic face, an idea came to her. Deciding that a little payback might be in order, she turned to her audience. "How would you all like to see him again?"

The audience erupted into wild applause just as she'd suspected they would. Making eye contact with Ian, she saw that the man was completely unwilling to venture back on the stage he'd occupied only yesterday.

How do you like it? she thought.

There was more than one way to skin a cat, Dakota

decided. Looking around, she caught the eye of the person she wanted. She signaled to one of the cameramen to train his camera at the wings.

Perforce, Ian, looking very solemn, was captured on one of the monitors. All attention was focused there, including Ian's.

Gotcha.

"And there he is, ladies," she told her audience gleefully. "My six-foot shadow for the next two weeks." They were just about to introduce the first guest, the holdover from yesterday's show, when hands throughout the audience suddenly shot up. They'd already dispensed with the question-and-answer segment of the program.

Dakota decided to make an exception. "We only have time for one question before we start," she told them, looking around. "You, the lady in the yellow."

A perky looking woman in her midtwenties bounced up to her feet. "Yesterday you told the audience that having someone around like that would drive you crazy. How are you liking it so far?"

Liking was hardly the word she would have used. Dakota took a breath before answering. "I'm adjusting," she finally said diplomatically.

"Yeah, I would, too," some unknown woman called out. Her comment received hoots and laughter.

Dakota glanced back toward Ian. He was standing in the shadows; otherwise, she had a feeling he would be turning deep red right now.

* * *

She put in a full day, staying at the studio longer than usual. There were new promos to shoot for the upcoming week and lists of guests for the next month to approve. By the time she finally left the studio, dusk had come and gone and evening was wrapping itself firmly around the city that never slept.

It might not, but she was certainly ready to, she thought.

Ian walked beside her in the parking garage. Most of the people had already left. The sound of their footsteps echoed eerily back to her. She had to admit that just this one instance, it was nice having someone with her. She wasn't normally afraid, but she wasn't as reckless as he thought, either. The close-to-empty parking facility was making her a little uneasy.

Probably his power of suggestion, she thought defensively. Until he'd gotten started with his "look before you leap" philosophy, she wouldn't have given any thought to coming down here at this time of night.

Maybe you should. Maybe he's right.

And maybe she was just too tired to make any sense.

As if picking up on the word that was echoing in her brain, Ian commented, "You look tired."

They came to her automobile, and she paused at the driver's side, hitting the automatic release. "I am, a little."

He opened the door for her. "Want me to drive?"

About to say no, she changed her mind. She wasn't averse to being pampered. "Okay."

As she got in on the passenger side, she had a feeling that, for once, Ian approved of her choice. She buckled up and closed her eyes.

As if she cared.

When they got out of the elevator, Ian preceded her down the hall. He used his own key to unlock the door.

"Afraid it might be booby-trapped?" she asked.

He pocketed the key, opening the door for her. "No, just being polite."

She felt like an idiot. "Sorry."

Maybe she was being too edgy. Once in her apartment, Dakota stepped out of her shoes and let the plush carpet caress the bottoms of her feet for a second. "Sure you don't want to go home for the night?" she asked.

He flipped on the switch beside the door. The chandelier flooded the foyer with light. Some of it seeped out into the living room. "My suitcase is already here."

"It can go with you. I'm sure it wouldn't mind."

He could feel her staring at the back of his head. Turning around to face her, he could almost touch the questions that were forming in her mind. "What?"

"Don't you have a life?" she asked. "Isn't there a Mrs. Bodyguard waiting for you?"

He thought of his ex. After they'd broken up, he'd had no desire to put himself back on the market again. Going out took investing yourself, and that just wasn't him. "No."

He'd told her about his ex-wife, but he hadn't told her anything about his current status. "A potential Mrs. Bodyguard?"

"No."

"So this is it for you?" She shook her head, unwilling to believe he was selling himself so short. After all, the man did have a great deal of potential. "You have no life, no dreams, no aspirations?"

He thought of unstrapping his service revolver. If this was home, he would have already taken it off. But he was on the job. Twenty-four/seven according to the agreement. That meant the gun remained part of his wardrobe.

"My dream, as you call it," he told her, "is to have a world where people can go about their business without the risk of someone cutting them down." He did slip off his jacket. "Until that day, I'll work on the problem one client at a time."

She tried not to notice his handgun. Guns didn't make her nervous; they never had. But it just served to remind her about the role he was playing. And the one she was supposed to take on.

Sleepiness was beginning to be replaced by something else. She found herself standing beside him, looking up. Had she gotten into his space or he into hers? She wasn't sure. All she did know was that she felt an unsettling flutter in her stomach. Again.

"Want to play poker?"

"Not particularly."

She decided to push just a little. "If I tell you to play poker…?"

He gave her a long, steady look before he apparently surrendered. "Where do you keep the cards?"

She held her hand to stop him. "That's okay, it was a test." She was definitely too close, she thought. Time for distance again. "I think I'll just go to bed."

"Good idea."

The words followed her down the hall.

She wasn't so sure about it being a good idea. She went to bed, but getting to sleep was another matter entirely. After the day she'd put in, she should have been tired, but she wasn't. She was wired. Wired like a highly lethal explosive.

Spinning around on her bed like a top didn't help matters, either.

Forty-five minutes later, muttering under her breath, she finally abandoned her bed. Grabbing a robe, she pulled it on and walked out of her bedroom. Maybe eating something would make her sleepy.

She went into the kitchen and found Ian sitting there. He had a deck of cards on the table. It was as if he'd been waiting for her. She looked at him quizzically.

"I figured you'd be back."

"How did you find the cards?"

"Looked in the most logical place."

The cards had been in her desk drawer in the den. That didn't strike her as a particularly logical place to look, but he was the expert at recovery, not her. Apparently with good results. Sitting down opposite him, she instructed, "Deal."

He did as she asked. Five cards went to each of them before he retired the deck to the table. He opened his hand very slowly, his eyes taking in each new symbol that was exposed. "I'd imagine you earn a pretty decent salary at what you do."

"Yes." She raised her eyes to his. Where was this going? Was he telling her to keep her bets low because she had more money than he did? Or was this some kind of fancy bluffing about to begin?

The question had been rhetorical. He knew exactly what she made, just as he'd known exactly what she ate for breakfast. He made it his business to know details, even if this wasn't a real assignment.

He continued looking at his hand. "So how is it you can't afford a nightgown?"

She looked down at the jersey that was peeking out from beneath her robe. It was the same one she'd worn the night before. "I tend to like this one. It has sentimental value."

"First boyfriend?"

She laughed. He'd guessed first instead of last, or college. "Damn, you're good. How did you know?"

He'd read the words on it the first time she'd worn it. The name of some high school out west was sewn along one sleeve. "Like you said, I'm good." And then he added, "It's my business to know. Jacks or higher to open."

She looked at her hand. One lone queen sat amid

four numbered cards. She folded the hand. "That lets me out."

He moved in a quarter. "But not me."

He was good at cards, too.

Chapter Eight

She'd purposely retreated right after breakfast, saying something about going to her room to work on some new ideas for the show. When he told her he'd be in his room if she needed him, she thought she might have a chance to get away with it. She had an appointment for nine-thirty with her gynecologist, and she really didn't feel like having him tag along.

Getting dressed, she quietly slipped out of her room and tiptoed past his. Her eyes on his closed door, she held her breath until she got into the foyer.

Where her escape was foiled. Ian stepped out of the den that was just off the foyer, a knowing look on his face. "Going somewhere?"

She drew her shoulders up. "Yes." From the jacket slung on his arm, she could see that he was ready to leave with her. "And you don't have to come along."

The protest fell on deaf ears, just as she knew it would. "That's the nature of the arrangement. I go where you go."

In desperation she exclaimed, "For pity's sake, it's a doctor visit."

A glimmer of what she took to be concern crossed his brow as he peered down at her. "You sick?"

"No," she snapped, and then added, "thanks for asking," in a more regular voice. Was there a way to appeal to his better side? "It's just an annual checkup. Very routine," she insisted. "You can stay here or go wherever it is that bodyguards go when they're not guarding."

Her words were still not having any effect. He was still walking her to the door. As he reached for the doorknob, Dakota paused, frustration bubbling up inside of her. Her bodyguard had already jogged with her this morning, and she supposed, in a perverse sort of way, she enjoyed having him there because he gave her someone to compete against.

But a sense of competition wasn't at issue here. More like annoyance. "You're not going to listen, are you?"

The look he gave her answered her question. "I get paid to use my judgment about dangerous situations."

Only self-control kept her from dropping her mouth open. "And you think my doctor is dangerous?"

He shook his head. The movement was infinitesimal

and all the more dramatic for it. "It's not your doctor, it's you."

Now he *really* wasn't making any sense to her. "*I'm* a danger to me?"

"In a way." He spoke evenly, deliberately, as if to a slow-witted child. It made her furious, and only training kept the emotion from exploding. "You're much too exposed, much too blasé about your safety."

She exhaled. How did people live like this on a regular basis? If she were in that kind of position, to feel that she needed to avail herself of the services of someone like Ian Russell, she would have gone crazy. As it was, strands of claustrophobia threatened to tighten themselves around her.

"I wasn't raised to live in a box, Russell. I like going out, I like mingling. I don't particularly like going to the doctor, but I like sharing the experience even less." She gave it one last try, although she could feel failure swiftly overtaking her. "Now, take a break for heaven's sake. You've been my bodyguard for over forty-eight hours, you've earned vacation time."

Very gently Ian ushered her out the door and then locked it behind them. Pocketing the key, he looked at her. "It doesn't work like that."

"It's not working at all," she complained under her breath. This was carrying things too far. The man was becoming absolutely infuriating. She walked into the elevator ahead of him. "Damn it, this is just a routine trip—"

"If you had a stalker or a potential kidnapper," Ian said

quietly, "he wouldn't just back away because this was a 'routine' visit to your doctor. He'd use the opportunity to observe you or get close to you—" he looked down into her face, his gray eyes very somber "—or possibly even abduct you. It's my job to see that never happens."

God, what a grim picture he painted. She rolled her eyes. "Is it your job to drive me crazy?"

The express elevator brought them to the underground garage. "That would come under 'fringe benefits.'"

She stopped to look at him. "Your sense of humor picks the oddest times to surface."

"It didn't," he replied mildly.

She wasn't sure if he was being serious or not. Everything else he'd said so far had been. She strode over to where her car was parked. "How do you stand it?" she asked.

"Stand what?" There was just the faintest curve of his lips, or maybe she just imagined it. "You?"

"No. How do you stand living in such a negative world?" She shivered at the very idea of it. "In a world where you're constantly waiting for bad things to happen?"

He opened her door for her, then rounded the hood and got in on the passenger side. "I don't wait for bad things to happen," he corrected. "With luck, I prevent them from happening." He buckled up. "So far, I've been lucky."

Her belt secure, she put the key in the ignition. Dakota sensed that crime prevention was more important to this silent man than as a way of earning his pay. She sensed that ensuring no one was harmed on his watch was a point of honor with him.

After starting the car, she backed out of her space. Within a minute they were on the road. And stopped at a light.

"Okay, I get it and I understand it." She looked at him before putting her foot back on the accelerator. "But could you be a little less, oh, I don't know, robotic about it? I feel like I'm being shadowed by the Terminator."

"Being a bodyguard is serious business."

She'd had it up to here with serious. "But we're just pretending, remember?"

He waited until they were stopped at the next light before answering. "I don't know how to pretend."

That was becoming painfully obvious, Dakota thought as she made a right turn at the next corner.

The doctor she was seeing had his office within Lennox Hill Hospital. Traffic kept the drive from being reasonable. She didn't throw herself on Ian's mercy until after she found parking and was entering the hospital. "The doctor's office is on the sixth floor. His exam room only has one way out."

The elevator car was crammed with visitors. He sidled over to one side, making sure that she was buffered between his body and the elevator wall. "Why are you telling me this?"

She struggled against the pink hue of embarrassment. Born and raised within the film community, she was not nearly as blasé about things as she would have liked to be. "So that you understand you don't have to go in with me."

The first stop was the sixth floor. Taking her arm to usher her out, Ian nodded as they made their way out of the elevator. "Understood."

She could have sworn there was a hint of a smile along his lips, but she wasn't altogether certain.

Ian discovered there wasn't much for a man to read inside of a gynecologist's office. He kept his mind occupied by doing calculations in his head. Dakota wasn't taken in until fifteen minutes after her appointment and finally emerged another half hour later. He was on his feet the moment she stepped back into the waiting room.

After opening the door for her, he fell into step beside her. "Everything okay?"

She hadn't had to open a single door since he had come into her life. She supposed there were worse things to put up with. Her independence had never gone so far as to demand that she be allowed to push every door she came in contact with. "Other than the fact that I seemed to have developed an annoying growth on my side, yes."

He pressed for the elevator, then shoved his hands into his pockets. "Don't worry. It'll be gone in less than two weeks."

"One can only hope."

She waited until they were wandering through the parking structure before she said anything further. "Look, Russell, it's nothing personal—"

"Being a bodyguard never is." He vaguely moved his shoulders in a half shrug.

Intrigued with what he'd just said, she forgot about her intended apology. "You mean you never get involved with your clients?"

As they walked, Ian scanned the scene. For the most part, the area was deserted, with only a handful of cars parked on this level. "Other than to know their routines and be there to protect them, no."

She didn't believe him. Dakota pushed the issue. "If you were my bodyguard, would you take a bullet for me?"

"Yes."

He'd answered her without a second's hesitation. It took a special man to agree to such sacrifice. "That's pretty personal, wouldn't you say?"

"It's my job."

As far as she was concerned, there was only one instance in which that was an acceptable part of a job description. And it didn't apply to her. "I'm not the president."

"No, you're someone who's paying for protection," he told her simply. Continuing to walk, they went down to the next level. "You deserve to get it."

She kept to the right as a car passed them, going deep into the bowels of the structure. "What about that woman who keeps calling you?" She glanced back over her shoulder at him. "Alexis, I think I heard you say."

There was no "think" about it. From a very young age, she had always been able to absorb what was going on around her like a dry sponge. The woman had called Ian three times in her presence. Dakota didn't doubt that there had been more calls from the needy woman.

"She has a few delusion problems." Ian's response was guarded.

Was he like that with all his clients? she wondered. Dakota was curious to see if she could get him to open up, to register some kind of emotion. "Like thinking that her bodyguard is in love with her?"

He spotted her vehicle and approached it. "I never gave her any cause to think that."

"How close did you get?" Testing the waters, or maybe herself, Dakota moved closer to him. She saw something flicker in his eyes and found herself enjoying it. She never pushed what her grandfather had once referred to as "womanly wiles," but there was something about this tall, stoic centurion who'd temporarily been forced into her life that made her a little reckless. She wasn't unaware of the attraction that hummed between them. Taking a deep breath, leaving less than a teardrop's space between them, she asked, "This close?"

She was in his space. Having her less than a hair's breadth away was scrambling his insides and pinching his gut to the point that breathing was a challenge.

"No," Ian said, placing his hands on her shoulders and deliberately moving her away. "More like this close."

Her eyes held him fast. "What are you afraid of, Ian?"

His answer surprised her. She'd expected him to

gruffly declare, "Nothing." Wasn't that what macho men did? Pretended to be fearless? Instead, he looked at her and said. "You."

Dakota blinked, wondering if she'd heard wrong. "Me?"

He told himself to get into the car, to place the stick shift between them, but he remained where he was. "Yes. Women like you tend to mess with a man's mind, make him forget things."

Cars beeped as they drove by. It was all noise to her, melding into the background. Dakota felt an undercurrent of something she couldn't quite describe going on between them. Drawing her to him. Making her wonder, not for the first time, what it would be like to have this man kiss her.

"Maybe that's a good thing once in a while," she said slowly, watching his lips. Wondering. "Might make a man realize there's more out there than just work."

"There's a hell of a lot more things out there than just work." For a second Ian could feel himself weakening. Could feel himself wanting to give in.

But life wasn't about giving in. It was about assuming positions and maintaining them. He had to maintain his. "But not for me." He got into the car, then looked out at her. "Aren't you going to be late for the show?"

She didn't care about being late. She wanted this damn frustration thing to leave her. It was like some kind of strange itch and she didn't like it. Didn't like, too, being the only one who felt it.

"Right," she mumbled as she got in on the driver's side. Buckling up, she started the car again and peeled out of the spot more than a tad too fast.

"Ease up, no point in breaking the sound barrier," he told her.

Oh, but there was a point, she thought. She was trying to outrace the itch.

That night, when they returned from the studio, Ian fully expected the evening to be more or less a carbon copy of the other two nights that had transpired so far. So when he saw her emerge from her room dressed in a little black dress, whose slightly flared skirt swirled and flirted along the tops of her thighs, Ian dropped the book he'd been reading. His favorite author's new offering could wait. Business always came first.

Instinct had him on his feet, reaching for the jacket he'd slung over the back of the easy chair. He was right behind her as she made her way to the foyer. "Where are you going?"

Dakota checked the contents of her small purse, then snapped it shut. Taking the black, three-quarter-length coat off the coatrack, she began to slip it on. Her answer was a single word. "Out."

Ingrained habit had him moving behind her in order to help her on with the coat. The exchange, he thought, sounded like one that took place inside of many homes, usually between a parent and a swiftly exiting teenager. Except that they were neither. "Where 'out'?"

"Out," she repeated. It had been years since she'd been subjected to inquisitions as she tried to make her getaway. Her mother had been lenient, but her father had been relentless. She turned to look at Ian. "If you must know, I'm going club hopping with MacKenzie." She reached for the doorknob. "Don't wait up."

But he was right there with her, throwing on his coat, shadowing her footsteps. "I won't have to."

She stopped hurrying. Suddenly there no longer was a need to. "I need to unwind."

"I won't get in your way."

He already was in her way. He was *constantly* in her way. And he was the reason she needed to unwind in the first place.

"The hell you won't."

But even as she said it, she knew there was no way around it. Apparently no matter what she said, her dark warrior was coming along.

The wall of noise intensified the moment they walked inside the darkened nightclub. The swirling lights emitted a rainbow of color that moved about the area like a hurricane.

Dakota felt his grasp on her arm as she tried to make her way through the crowd, searching for MacKenzie.

Her friend spotted them first. Standing up at the tiny table she'd secured for herself and Dakota, she waved madly until Dakota saw her. She sat back down, amusement in her eyes as she watched her friend and Ian work their way toward her.

In Dakota's estimation, Zee looked happier to see Ian than her. "Hey, I see you brought your shadow. Hi, Ian." MacKenzie's voice was the last word in cheer. "I'm sorry, there were only two chairs."

"No problem," he told her. After issuing a strong, nonverbal warning as he glanced at Dakota, Ian went in search of a third chair.

Dakota sank down opposite MacKenzie. She leaned into the other woman and said between semiclenched teeth, "This is getting very old."

MacKenzie hadn't stopped looking at the man who'd come in with Dakota since his arrival. "I don't care what you say, I still think he's cute. Coming *and* going," she added wickedly.

"That has nothing to do with it, although I have no use for good-looking men—"

"I do," MacKenzie sighed.

Dakota didn't hear her. "The man is entirely too overbearing."

"He's supposed to be. It's the deluxe package, remember?"

Dakota shifted on the small chair, trying to get comfortable. She shed her coat, letting it fall back onto the back of the chair.

"One person's deluxe is another person's torture." Slowly taking in the surrounding area, she became aware that a handsome thirtyish man stood at her elbow.

The next moment, he leaned his hands on the back of her chair, his face close to hers. "Hi, beautiful, want to dance?"

"She doesn't," Ian informed him firmly. Having returned with his prize, Ian deposited the chair right next to where the other man stood.

The man jumped back. Half a head shorter, he looked properly intimidated by Ian. "Hey, sorry, didn't know you were together." His hands raised in surrender, he backed away.

Dakota felt a burst of fury go off inside her chest. Not that she was interested in the man's advances, but she resented Ian thinking he had the right to chase anyone away from her. What if she had been interested?

She turned on Ian. "Do you know why people go club hopping?"

Clubbing had never been his idea of fun. This club had particularly loud music. Any kind of prolonged contact was enough to jar his teeth loose. "Because they want to lose their hearing at an early age?"

She ignored the flippant remark. "To connect with other people."

He slid onto his chair. "So connect."

Dakota pressed her lips together. "With people they didn't know before they arrived."

He shook his head. "Bad idea."

Of course he'd say that. She ignored the amused expression on MacKenzie's face. "Do you ever have any fun?" Dakota asked.

His eyes held hers for a moment, and if her life had depended on it, she couldn't have read what was going on in his mind. "I'm having it now."

Dakota sighed, shaking her head. She made eye contact with MacKenzie. "Note to self—kill Alan in the morning."

"Alan didn't put him there, your fans did," MacKenzie reminded her.

"Alan's the one who got the studio to pay double."

MacKenzie rested her head on her upturned palm and fluttered her lashes at Ian. It was evident by the expression on the man's face, he didn't know what to make of her. "I'd say he was worth every penny."

"If I was paying for the privilege of being annoyed, yes." Rising to her feet, Dakota declared, "I'm going to get us something to drink." She glanced at Ian, "A can of oil for you, I presume."

"Just water." He was on his feet, too.

"No, stay," she ordered. Hand on his chest, she pressed him back down into his chair. "Stay here with MacKenzie and guard her for a minute." She pointed over to the bar which was a large fifteen-foot rectangle. "You can watch me walk all of twenty feet to the bar," she told him. "Close enough for you to leap into action if you have to." And with that she walked away.

MacKenzie beckoned Ian to lean forward. When he did, she said, "I've never seen her this edgy before. I don't know if you bring out the best in her or the worst."

He never took his eyes off the woman as she made her way to the bar. Even with so many bodies between them, Dakota still stood out. Ian sighed inwardly. He had his work cut out for him.

"Probably a little of both."

Dakota absorbed the noise and the crowd around the long, sleek bar. The electric-blue overhead lighting added a surreal glow to the immediate area. What she'd told Ian earlier was true. She just wanted to unwind, and he wasn't letting her.

Raising her hand, she managed to catch the bartender's eye after a moment. The man, chosen for his skill as well as his overt good looks, lost no time in coming over to take her order.

"Two strawberry daiquiris and a beer," she said. Maybe a beer would help loosen Ian up, she thought. Something had to. She didn't think she could bear another week and a half of this.

She moved as someone wedged his way in on her right. "I'll pay for what the lady's having," a deep voice said. Surprised and about to demur, Dakota turned to see a tall, attractive, blond-haired man in his early thirties giving her the once-over. He had nice brown eyes, she thought. "I know this sounds like a line, but you look awfully familiar."

"I'm on television."

"No kidding." Leaning an elbow on the bar, he seemed properly impressed. His eyes swept over her. "Would I have seen you?"

Natural inbred modesty made her laugh. "Only if you watch daytime television."

He shook his head. "I'm afraid my boss frowns on that kind of thing. I work on Wall Street, and watching TV cuts into profits." Smiling genially, he put his hand out. "Eric Simon."

She slipped her hand into his. "Dakota Delany."

She watched him for a sign of recognition, but there was none.

"Nice name." He made himself comfortable around her. "So, what are you doing for the rest of the evening, Dakota Delany?" The man took out his wallet and paid for the drinks as the bartender placed them on the bar.

Despite what she'd said to Ian, she didn't come to the bar with the idea of meeting men. Certainly not with the idea of abandoning her companions for one. "I'm with friends."

He reached behind her, and after a beat she felt his hand lightly on her waist. Friendly yet not too familiar. "I can be a friend."

Maybe he could at that, but not while she was with the chaperon from hell. She moved to the side. "No, I don't think that I—"

And then suddenly Ian was there between them. The next thing happened so fast, it only registered after the fact.

Ian punched Eric out.

Chapter Nine

Shock and disbelief raced through Dakota as she watched Eric Simon sink like a stone to the floor. Anger at Ian flared immediately. To add to the confusion, camera flashes went off all around her. As with every popular hot spot in New York, paparazzi hid in the woodwork, waiting for opportunities just like this. A picture was still worth a thousand words, and these days, sometimes an equal amount in hard cash.

And Ian had presented them with one golden opportunity on a silver platter.

Dakota grabbed hold of Ian's arm in case he was going to take another swing at the incapacitated man.

Like an avenging angel, she placed herself in between Ian and the fallen Eric.

"Are you out of your mind?" she demanded hotly. "He was just talking to me."

Unruffled by her anger, Ian looked down at the man he'd just hit. The latter, still on the floor, was groggy but conscious. "He was doing more than that."

"Okay, he had his hand around my waist, that didn't mean he was going to have his way with me." Dakota knelt down to see what kind of damage her obviously deranged pretend bodyguard had done. By her estimation, Eric Simon was going to have some shiner by tomorrow. She felt a stab of guilt. In a way this was her fault. "I'm a big girl." She looked up at Ian, fury in her eyes. He had no right to act like some Neanderthal protector. "I can take care of myself."

"Not when you're drugged."

The stark words hung in the air between them. He offered her a hand and she rose to her feet. "What are you talking about?"

Ian nodded toward the man he'd just hit. "I saw him slip something into your drink." Ian indicated the daiquiri that was closest to her on the bar, then glared at the other man. "What was it, punk?"

Rubbing his jaw, Eric Simon slowly gained his feet. He watched Ian warily, real fear in his eyes. "Just a little 'E' to enhance the lady's ultimate pleasure, that's all."

Dakota even abstained from aspirin unless absolutely necessary. Her eyes widened in shock as she swung around to look at Eric. "You tried to drug me?" The look of helplessness on Eric's face was all she needed to confirm Ian's accusation.

Without thinking, she let loose with a punch, connecting with Eric's chin. He went down as quickly as he'd come up. More flashes went off. The crowd that had gathered around them closed in a little more, eating away at the semicircle of space they'd allotted the central trio in this drama.

Ian nodded his approval, effectively masking any surprise that he might have felt. Looked like Dakota Delany could take care of herself after all.

Their eyes locked. "Not bad," Ian said. He took out his cell phone and pressed a single digit.

Dakota rubbed her knuckles, seething at what Eric had presumed to do. And shaking inwardly at what might have happened had Ian not been looking out for her.

Great, she thought, this is going to make the man impossible. She realized that he was on the phone. Now what? "Who are you calling?"

Faced with a crime, the cop in him had been quick to surface. "Last time I heard, trying to drug someone, especially with an illegal substance, was against the law." Instantly some of the crowd melted away from them and into the background, taking whatever substance they might have been abusing with them.

Panic marred Eric Simon's near perfect features. "Hey, there's no call for that," he protested, attempting to scramble to his feet a second time. "It was all just in fun."

Dakota saw red. She took a step toward him, unconsciously fisting her hand again. "You want fun? I'll show you fun."

Ian shifted so that his body was partially between the two. "I'd stay down if I were you," he advised Eric. "The lady looks like she means business."

And then a voice came on the other end of the line. Ian turned away from them to give the policeman, someone with whom he'd once worked the streets, the particulars of the incident.

MacKenzie put her arm around Dakota's shoulder. Suddenly remembering that she was there, Dakota glanced at her and saw concern in the woman's face.

"Are you okay?" MacKenzie asked.

"Yeah." She was a lot better than she could have been, Dakota thought humbly. Nothing like this had ever happened to her before. "Just a little thrown, that's all."

MacKenzie took her hand in both of hers and examined her knuckles. "That's going to bruise," she predicted.

"It'll give Albert someplace new to apply makeup," Dakota quipped.

Looking over MacKenzie's head, she frowned at the gathering. Camera flashes kept popping, coming from all directions. Exasperated, she covered her face, but there seemed to be no place to turn in order to get away from the persistent photographers.

MacKenzie's expression told her that her best friend knew exactly what was going through her mind. "Look at the bright side, at least you'll have something to tell the audience tomorrow."

"Yeah, right. They'll probably read it in the entertainment section of the *Times* first," Dakota muttered.

As she sunk her head in her hands, she thought she heard something. Listening, she detected the wail of sirens in the background, cutting through the noise at the club. The music had stopped, but the lights continued to swirl, casting wild rainbows into every darkened corner of the place. The sirens grew louder. She looked at Ian and guessed he'd been the one to call the police.

Ian placed his body between her and some of the more eager photographers. "You want to wait in the car?" he suggested to her.

"No," she countered, "I want to go home." And she did. As much as she'd wanted to get out before, that was how much she wanted to leave now. But she knew it was impossible.

She thought she saw a hint of compassion on Ian's face, but that could have been a trick of the lighting. "Right after the police take your statement."

Restless, edgy, she didn't know what to do with all the different emotions running through her, struggling for domination. In an unbridled moment she looked at Ian accusingly. "You know, this never happened to me before I went out with you."

"You two dating now, Dakota?" A voice from somewhere behind all the flashes called out the query.

"He's my bodyguard." The response came without

thought. God knew she didn't want to be painted as paired off with anyone.

"Lucky for you you've got one," a girl with tinted pink hair and serious eyes said to her as she leaned back against the bar.

"Yeah," Dakota muttered, feeling anything but that. "Lucky."

It felt like a century instead of three hours since she'd left the apartment. She flipped on the light and kicked off her shoes. The policemen who had arrived in response to Ian's call had been polite and tried to hurry things along, but even so, she'd had to take a ride to the police station in order to give her full statement. Ian came along not just as her bodyguard but to add his piece of the story. Only MacKenzie had been free to go home. From her vantage point, the other woman hadn't actually witnessed anything other than the haymaker Ian had awarded the would-be rapist.

Checking the lock, Ian turned toward her. "You really should get that security system installed."

"Right." She sighed, not wanting to get into yet another discussion about safety. She blew out a breath. "I guess I should thank you."

He wasn't in it for the thanks. Had he been independently wealthy, he still would have gotten into this line of work. It needed doing.

Ian shrugged carelessly. "Like you said, you can take care of yourself." And then he looked at her knuckles, which were slightly swollen. "You'd better get some ice on that." Even as he said it, he began walking into the kitchen to fetch the ice. "That's a nice right cross you have."

She flushed at the compliment as she followed him. "One of the stuntmen on Grandpa's show gave me a few pointers the summer I turned sixteen." That had been the summer she'd suddenly blossomed—a late bloomer, her mother had called her. Her grandfather worried that boys would try to take advantage of her and insisted she learn a few moves to keep her from harm.

Sliding onto a chair, she placed her right hand on the table. Ian brought over two ice cubes wrapped in a paper towel and gently applied them to the bruised area. She tried not to wince as the wet paper came in contact with her skin.

She raised her eyes to his.

Why did this feel so intimate? It was just ice. He would have done the same thing for a wounded puppy, she thought. And yet...

"I wasn't going to let him pick me up, you know," she heard herself saying.

"Uh-huh."

"I wasn't," she insisted. "I just wanted to get out for a little while, but I'm not an idiot." His expression remained unchanged. Her voice rose a little. "I don't believe in looking across a crowded room, making eye contact and hearing violins."

With ice leaking on one side, he flipped over and

placed that side against her knuckles. "Doubt if you could in that place."

Dakota frowned. "You know what I mean."

Yes, he knew what she meant and he didn't want to know anything else. The less he knew about her personally, the better chance he had of keeping this on a professional level. "You don't have to explain yourself to me."

"I'm not explaining myself," she snapped, then shut her mouth as she took a deep breath. "Okay, I am explaining myself, but only because I don't want you thinking—"

He headed her off before she said something that might embarrass them both. "What I think doesn't matter."

The interruption only served to annoy her. "Will you please stop contradicting me? You are the most perverse human being—"

"You know, it's not necessary to have everyone think well of you."

"It is if I can help it." How had he known that about her? she wondered, irritated. "Damn, you have me all tied up in knots and confused." A pin fell from her hairdo, and she put it on the table. "This is all your fault in a way, you know."

"How so?"

The expression on his face was mild. He was humoring her. Dakota felt like beating on him with her fists, but that would only aggravate her bruised knuckles.

"If I hadn't been so intent on getting some space between us—"

"You would have had eyes in the back of your head?" he guessed. "That was how that creep slipped that substance into your drink, just before he put his arm around your waist. The drink was on the bar behind you." And had there not been a mirror set at such a angle that he saw what the man was doing, Ian thought, he might not have been able to save her.

Both she and MacKenzie were to have daiquiris. There was no guarantee she would have had the one on the end. "He could have wound up drugging MacKenzie," she realized, horrified.

Ian nodded, shifting the wrapped ice cube pack yet again. "The guy took a chance. But from his point of view, he had nothing to lose."

She intended to be at the man's arraignment bright and early tomorrow. "He will if I can help it. Scum like that shouldn't be allowed to roam free." Rising, she flexed her knuckles. They felt stiff and achy already.

Ian stood and tossed the partly melted ice cubes into the sink. He nodded at her hand. "That's going to feel worse tomorrow."

She'd gotten more than one fracture as a tomboy and knew what to expect. "Not as bad as I would have felt if that creep had gotten away with what he was trying to do." Rather than leave the room, she crossed to him and impulsively brushed a kiss against Ian's cheek. "Thank you."

The words, softly uttered, hung between them as Ian looked at her. She'd caught him completely off guard.

Those same stirrings that had been invading and haunting him these last few days increased in magnitude, threatening to overwhelm him. He'd banked them down before, but this time they proved more difficult to hide away.

Impossible, actually.

Especially since, after kissing his cheek, Dakota didn't retreat, didn't even stop balancing on her toes, moving out of range.

Her lips were very close, very accessible to his.

The next happened as if it had been scripted somewhere. But not by him. He wasn't given to impulse, not unless he was on the job, covering his partner's back, reacting by instincts. Just the way he had while watching Dakota tonight in that nightclub, he realized. Then gut instincts had completely taken over.

Like now.

His hand spanning so that it partially framed her cheek, he cupped it ever so lightly as he brought his lips down to hers. He did it even as something inside of him ordered *Stop!*

He didn't listen.

The noise from the nightclub was still partially throbbing in his ears. But not so loudly that he couldn't hear the pounding of his heart.

Or maybe he just felt the rhythm so acutely it seemed he was hearing it. All he really knew was that kissing her felt wonderful.

Blood rushed through his veins the way it did whenever he entered an area blindly, unsure of the outcome.

Every single nerve ending in his body was at attention. And absorbing the exhilarating pleasure that flooded every part of his body.

Wow. Oh, wow.

The refrain echoed through Dakota's brain as the kiss he'd started deepened, taking possession of her, sweeping her off her feet at lightning speed. Without thinking, she leaned her bottom into his. Almost sealing it to his. Heat and warm thoughts came rushing at her from all directions, making her yearn.

Making her want him to want her.

Making her want him.

Almost outside her own body, she twined her arms around his neck, letting herself go further than she would have expected. Her whole body was quickening.

Waiting.

And then, suddenly unsure of herself, afraid of what she could be getting into, Dakota drew back. She pressed her lips together, tasting him. Tasting desire and feeling fear mingle in with it. She'd been here before, in this land of lightning bolts and tidal waves. Been here and then been cast adrift.

"Um, hold it a second. This is happening a little too fast. I—"

Rather than press, she was surprised to have him follow her lead. "My fault," Ian acknowledged, backing away.

It wasn't what she wanted to hear. A prisoner of confusion and scrambled emotions, she could feel irritation mounting. "No, damn it, it's not your 'fault.'" Did he think she was some kind of child, to be swept away by any man's will? She was her own person, not some man's puppet. "There you go again, making it seem as if I'm some kind of helpless little dolt—"

Without thinking, Ian touched his fingers to his lips. Unaware of what the simple action did to the woman watching him. "No, I wouldn't call you a helpless little dolt."

"You didn't take advantage of me or the moment," she insisted.

"Okay."

The single word only served to inflame her further. "I wanted to kiss you as much as you wanted to kiss me." She watched a corner of his mouth rise ever so slightly. He was still humoring her. She wasn't getting through to him, damn it. What did it take? "Nothing happens to me that I don't want to happen."

He raised his hands in mock surrender. "Got it. You're independent."

"Damn straight I am."

And then, as if to prove it, she threw away the life preserver that was securely around her. For all the world, Dakota felt as if she was on some kind of roller-coaster ride and couldn't find a way to get off. She'd never behaved like this around anyone else, never felt like this around anyone else. Just what kind of buttons did this man press with her?

Desperate to prove her independence, she stepped back into the ring of fire.

This time *she* kissed *him*. Kissed him as if she was executing some kind of payback.

The moment she did, she immediately lost herself. She was free-falling. It was as if she'd opened a door and, rather than stepping out onto a balcony, found nothing beneath her feet except space. The air in her lungs backed up as she went plunging down a ravine.

Dakota held on for dear life as she felt her blood surging through her veins, heard some kind of wild rushing noise in her ears. She was hotter than she could ever recall outside of the one time she'd had the flu that first spring in college. But even that fever had been mild compared to the one consuming her right now.

Ian could feel his body priming, could feel himself wanting her. He never crossed this kind of line with a client. Ever. He was supposed to behave professionally, not like some smitten idiot fresh out of a monastery.

Which, in a way, he was.

He'd kept himself so busy with work, he couldn't remember the last time he'd made love with a woman. No one had to tell him that having his wife walk out on him had left a devastating mark. Part of him had thought he could do without women.

That part stood corrected.

But it couldn't be this woman. This woman was vulnerable, and no matter what she said to the contrary, if he pressed, if they wound up making love the way every bone in his body was begging him to, he'd be doing nothing short of taking advantage of her.

Like that scum cooling his heels in the holding pen at the police station.

Hands on her shoulders, Ian drew his head back and gently created space between them. It cost him more than he'd thought it would. But honor didn't come cheaply.

Her lips looked slightly swollen. Something quickened inside of him, urged him to give in. He held fast to his position, even as it threatened to slip out of his hands.

"I think maybe it's time to go to bed."

Dakota wanted him to take her, to kiss her again until she was utterly mindless. She wanted him to carry her off so that she could pretend—to herself—that she wasn't really to blame. That it was just one of those things that happened between a man and a woman. She didn't want common sense intervening.

She took in a breath and looked up at him. Her mind was as clear as the harbor when a low-lying fog crept in. "What?"

Adorable. Now, there was a word that hardly ever crossed his mind, he thought, but it was applicable when used to describe the expression on her face. Adorable. "Separately."

"Oh." Disappointment crashed in on her. She blinked, trying to focus. The clouds in her brain remained. "Right."

Stung, hurt, afraid of saying anything that might give

her feelings away, she turned and walked away from him on shaky legs.

And slept not at all the entire night.

Chapter Ten

Awkwardness was not within her normal repertoire, yet that was what she felt the moment she went into the kitchen the next morning. Ian was there on the phone, making breakfast while he spoke in low tones to someone on the other end of the line.

Who? she wondered as she stopped in the doorway. His partner? Or some woman? Was the latter the reason he didn't want to follow the natural path that was laid out for them last night?

Straining and holding her breath, she found she still couldn't hear.

My God, I'm jealous. Jealous about some bodyguard cloned out of rock.

She really had fallen over the edge, Dakota thought, annoyed with herself. Damn it, it didn't matter who he was talking to. Why should she care? In another week, this man with his piercing glance would be out of her life and this ridiculous charade would be over.

She nodded curtly at him as she took the coffee he'd prepared. She tried to wrap herself up in everything but thoughts of him.

Of course, it didn't work.

It was a long day, made longer by the fact that she'd gotten next to no sleep the night before. Added to the irritation caused by sleeplessness had been her audience's glee over the story featured not only inside the entertainment section, but also on the front page of the local news section. MacKenzie had brought it to her attention just before they'd gone on the air. The caption had read: Talk Show Hostess Does More Than Talk and it had featured a photograph of her decking the creep who'd slipped the drug into her drink.

The second she'd emerged on the set, wild applause exploded. It escalated until she found herself the recipient of a standing ovation.

She'd glanced back to see Ian's reaction, but as always, he looked stoic. That, too, irritated her. Didn't anything register with this man on a personal level?

Had he felt nothing at all when they'd kissed last night? She'd forced herself to push the question away.

The question-and-answer segment of her program

threatened to take over the whole show if she didn't call a halt to it. The audience's disappointment could be felt in the first few minutes of the day's major interview.

That hadn't been the worst of it.

Members of her family called the minute they'd read the story on the West Coast. Her cell phone was constantly ringing. First her father, who'd gotten the heads-up from a fellow newscaster, then her mother. That call was followed by her grandfather, who read about the incident in the paper. It made her grateful that she didn't have a large, extended family the way some people did.

Her brother, Paul, had been particularly testy because, in a fit of desperation, she'd shut off her cell for a while. That had apparently been just when he had begun trying to call her. Of them all, Paul was the one who was a little straitlaced. It occurred to her as she listened to him that he and Ian might hit it off very well if they ever met each other. Which they weren't going to do, she reminded herself.

"I thought you were above that kind of thing." Paul's voice had been nothing short of accusing. She knew he hated being embarrassed. Her older brother probably figured their free-spirited mother was his only liability in that department. Surprise.

Still, she'd expected support from her sibling, not an upbraiding. "Some guy tried to slip a drug into my drink. It could have happened to anyone."

"Most people don't get their photograph splattered all over the place when it does." Out of all of them, he was the one who had shunned the spotlight and notoriety as if it was a second calling. He was the exact opposite of their mother, who loved it. There had been a time when their mother would have gone bareback riding on an eagle if it would have gotten her attention. Paul paused, then asked, "Are you okay?"

At the show of concern, the dark thoughts she was having about him faded. "I'm fine."

She heard paper rustling on the other end. She wondered which story he'd read, but thought it best not to ask.

"Lucky that bodyguard you have was so alert," he commented.

"He's not my bodyguard." The protest was automatic. Unless you were being stalked, she saw no reason to have bought and paid for muscle tracing your every step—unless you were vain. "He's just an experiment."

She heard her brother clear his throat. "I think I'm probably better off not knowing what that means."

"Watch some of those tapes of the show you're always claiming you're making and maybe you'll get a clue." She knew Paul was busy at work while her show aired, but he was always saying that he was faithfully taping each episode.

"I've got to go, Dakota. Next time, try to be more careful."

She promised and hung up. She certainly had no intention of being reckless or punching out someone else. Her problem now was that she still couldn't shake the restlessness that had been humming through her all day. It seemed to grow as the day progressed.

By all rights, because she was so tired, she should have just gone straight to bed the second she walked into her apartment. The thought of making contact with her king-size bed and its soft satin comforter had loomed before her like a seductive goal all day long.

But as the day progressed, as one thing built on another, the thought of going home and sharing the space with just Ian again created a nervousness within her that seeped into the center of her exhaustion. The tension continued to grow until it infused her with a shot of energy or adrenaline or something along those lines.

And it had her accepting Jerry Cole's invitation to dinner in a moment of complete distraction, not to mention madness. Jerry had cornered her just after the show, before she'd had time to even begin preparing for the next day's program.

He might not have gotten to her if she'd been thinking straight, Dakota ruminated now.

Jerry wasn't awful. There was just no chemistry between them, even though he thought there was. But when he asked, she'd said yes, and now, as she walked into her apartment, she went straight for her closet to try to put on something that would trouble Ian but not arouse Jerry.

Not exactly an easy task.

She worked her way from one end of her closet to the other. Then, in another moment of weakness, she decided to sacrifice Jerry in order to get back at Ian. She chose one of her sexier dresses, an electric-blue dress that appeared simple on the hanger, gorgeous on her body as it clung to every inch of her, beguilingly tantalizing the imagination it had set off.

Dakota wasn't even sure why she was going through with this, other than the fact that she felt she needed a breather from this man who was all but hermetically sealed to her side. That and it was Friday. She liked unwinding on Fridays.

So why did she feel so damn wound up? she wondered as she quickly showered and reapplied her makeup. Things were going well. Except for that blip in the road caused by John, her life was on track. She had a wonderful career and a better family. If ever there was a candidate for contentment poster child, it should have been her.

But it wasn't.

She decided it was best not to explore that until she had more sleep under her belt.

"You have the night off," she declared as she walked into the living room.

There was a novel on the coffee table, awaiting his pleasure. The bookmark indicated that he was about halfway through the tome, a novel by James Michener. The man had to be a speed reader, she thought. Either that, or he skipped huge chunks of the book.

Right now, he was making notes in his black notebook. When she'd asked him about it the other day, he'd said simply that he kept a journal while on the job. Curiosity had eaten away at her. She wanted to know what, if anything, he wrote about her that was remotely of a personal nature. But the book, like his tongue, seemed to be kept under lock and key. When he wasn't making entries, the book was completely out of sight.

Ian glanced up, and only restraint had him keeping his eyes in his head. The woman could have accomplished just as much wrapping herself in electric-blue plastic wrap. Had there been a pencil in his hand, it would have found itself broken in two, a casualty of the surge he felt inside. As it was, he managed to bend his pen.

Still, he kept his voice steady. "The agreement is, I don't take nights off."

"I have a date," she told him. She watched his face for a reaction, hating herself for caring.

His expression never changed. "I know."

Of course he did. Why did she think it would be otherwise? Annoyed that he seemed so all right with it, she dug in.

"Dates usually mean two people, unless it's a group date, at which time an even number of people go. You might not know this but you alone are not an even number, hence, you're not coming."

There was just the slightest hint of a smile on his lips. "I'll be there, you just might not know it."

She blew out a breath. This definitely wasn't going the way she wanted it to. She wanted him to stay here—

and possibly sulk. But at the very least, she wanted to get away from him. Then maybe she could stop thinking about him and wondering why it had been so easy for him to walk away last night.

"Are you planning on wiring me?"

"If you ask me, you're already pretty wired." He leaned in to her, trying not to notice that she was wearing a sexier perfume than usual. One that made him want to slip back into the transgression he'd committed last night. It took effort not to visibly react, but he congratulated himself on holding firm. "Don't worry, I won't interrupt anything. I'll be discreet."

"How do I know you won't pop up in various disguises?"

He laughed then, a small, mirthless sound. "You watch too many bad movies."

Annoyed, stymied, she threw up her hands. "And I'm stuck in a bad nightmare."

His eyes met and held hers. "Are there good nightmares?"

Dakota didn't answer. Or maybe her huge sigh did her answering for her. Like an eleventh-hour savior, the doorbell rang. She began to cross to the door when Ian placed himself between her and her goal.

"I'll do it," he told her.

Exasperated, she raised her hands as she stepped back. "Knock yourself out."

Rather than ask who it was the way he'd told her to do, Ian opened the door. But then, given that he was eight inches taller and about a hundred pounds heavier, Ian was far more of a force to be reckoned with than she was. The look on Jerry's face certainly said as much.

The latter's brown eyes darted back and forth between them. "Is…is she ready?" he asked uncertainly.

He was *not* going to speak for her, Dakota thought. She deliberately slipped out around the barrier Ian had formed with his body. "I'm ready." Thinking this was not one of her better ideas, she still forced cheer into her voice.

"Um, is he going with us?" Jerry looked up at Ian, then back at her. The uncertainty on his face increased.

"Not exactly," Dakota responded. Grabbing her coat, she wrapped both her arms around one of his and drew him toward the elevator. "There's a hundred in it for you if you lose him," she whispered.

Jerry laughed nervously in response.

Dakota had a sinking feeling that they weren't going to lose Ian anytime soon.

They didn't.

Even though Ian had told her that he would be discreet, she was acutely aware of him the entire time. In the restaurant he was seated at a table for one twenty feet away. Close enough to spring into action if necessary. He'd said he'd be far away enough to give her some privacy. It wasn't enough, in her book.

She did her best to pretend that the tall, dark man wasn't there. It was like being on the edge of a forest fire with your back to it, pretending not to feel the heat.

Impossible.

The evening turned out to be relatively short. She and Jerry ate, made the smallest of talk, and before she knew it, she was back at her door, relieved that it was over, unhappy that she felt that way. Jerry was attractive and intelligent. Why couldn't she enjoy herself in his company? Why did she feel like yawning every two seconds?

She forced herself to appear reluctant to have the evening end.

"Would you like to come in?" she suggested once he'd brought her up to her penthouse apartment. For the moment, Ian still hadn't joined them. But she knew his absence was going to be short-lived. He was probably parking his car in the garage even now.

For a fleeting second, Jerry seemed tempted, but then shook his head. "I get claustrophobic with someone breathing down my neck."

She laughed shortly. "Welcome to the club." It hadn't been fair of her to say yes to Jerry. Not under these circumstances, and had they not been in place, she would never have thought of going out with him. Guilt strummed through her. "I'm sorry about this."

"Don't be. Maybe we can do it again sometime when you don't have to have a chaperon around."

"Russell isn't my chaperon," she insisted, "he's my bodyguard."

"In this case, same difference," Jerry countered.

He started to lean in to kiss her. She supposed she

owed him that much, although the thought of kissing Jerry left her cold. She braced herself. Just then the penthouse elevator doors opened and Jerry jumped back like a cat whose tail had been stepped on.

"Maybe a rain check." He took a couple of steps back. "Take care of yourself. See you Monday." Passing Ian on his way to the elevator, he nodded nervously. Ian inclined his head as the man got into the car.

"First floor's already pressed," he said, turning away.

Dakota glared at Ian as the elevator doors closed. "You scared him away."

"If you ask me, I did you a favor. The man's a loser."

She'd come to the same conclusion, but she wasn't about to concede the point. "What would you know about it?"

"It's my job to be able to read people, make quick judgments. You could do a lot better." Ian waited for her to enter, followed, then locked the door again. "You should be a little more discriminating in your choice of men."

"Look, I'm really getting tired of you telling me what to do."

He loosened his tie, then slipped it into his pocket before taking off the jacket. "I call them as I see them. That's part of the package."

"Is being irritating as hell part of the package, too?"

He saw the fire in her eyes and felt himself reacting to it again. To her again. When he'd gotten out of the elevator and seen that weasel about to kiss her, something inside of him almost snapped.

She was pressing his buttons. Buttons she didn't even know she had under her fingertips. Buttons that spelled disaster for him.

He admitted to himself that Dakota Delany was the first woman who had ever really rattled his cage, at least to this extent. Even his ex, Marla, hadn't. Not so that down was up and night was day. Not so that he was tempted to…

He shut the thought away.

Because of the way he was and the way he'd been raised, a part of him had always been unreachable. He'd been as open with his ex as he thought humanly possible. And because he was the way he was, that wasn't very far.

But Dakota was different. She made him feel different, think different. With this woman, he thought of doing crazy things, of being someone other than who and what he was.

She made him want to start fresh.

But that would mean risking everything. He would be putting himself in jeopardy at the center of an emotional earthquake—the last place he wanted to be.

"That's a fringe benefit," he reminded her.

Tossing her purse onto the sofa, she glared at him. "How is irritating the hell out of me a fringe benefit for me?"

"It's not." He laughed, and this time the sound was rich, rounded and she was in danger of getting lost in it. "It's a fringe benefit for me."

Becoming instantly four inches shorter as she kicked off her shoes, she shook her head. But the look of exasperation had faded from her eyes.

"Just when I begin to despair that you're nothing more than a robot with good skin work, you pull a sense of humor out of the hat on me." She ran a hand through her hair. It was late. Maybe she'd finally get that sleep she needed. "I'm going to the kitchen to get some coffee. You want some?"

Traces of sleepiness showed around her eyes. That pull he kept feeling refused to leave him alone, and it was getting harder and harder to resist. What he needed more than coffee was a shower. Preferably one with ice cubes.

"I thought you'd want to get some sleep."

Amusement curved the corners of her mouth. "I do."

"So you're drinking coffee," he said like a man searching for the sense and finding none.

"Coffee puts me to sleep," she told him innocently as she watched the confusion etched on his face.

"And night is day and day is night."

This time she grinned. "Hey, we all march to a different drummer." She waved her hand at him. "Look at you."

"What about me?" The question wasn't so much defensive as it was curious.

She rotated her shoulders, feeling an ache. Feeling more aware that he was watching her every move. Something warm and personal began to spill inside of her. "You spend your time in other people's lives, neglecting having one of your own because it's too scary."

Now Ian looked defensive. "Not that it's true, but who said you could analyze me?"

She lifted a single shoulder, then let it fall. The strap slipped down with it, and she tugged it back into place. "You scared off my date. I need some kind of diversion."

"He wouldn't have given you any kind of diversion. The man was more of a rodent than a human." He shook his head decisively. "He's not your type."

She raised her chin as she fisted her hands at her waist defiantly. "Oh, and what's my type? You?"

The look he gave her turned her tongue to cotton. "More than he is."

Still, she wasn't about to capitulate so easily. There was a stand to be made here, although what kind and for what reason seemed to escape her. But she couldn't have him thinking that she walked around, waiting for him to indicate that he was interested in her.

She didn't want him to be interested in her, she insisted silently.

The hell she didn't.

But Dakota had never been one to give up without a fight. "At least he ran off because he was afraid of you. You ran off because you were afraid of me."

"I wasn't afraid of you," Ian informed her darkly.

"Okay then, what were you afraid of?"

How she came to be in his arms, he wasn't altogether sure. All he knew was that one moment they were verbally sparring, creating a chasm between them, the next moment his arms were around her and he was looking down into her face. The air stood still in his lungs.

For one brief instant, the barriers inside of him, the ones that kept all of his emotions so carefully dammed up, cracked right down the middle, allowing his feelings into the light of day.

"Me."

Chapter Eleven

Desire instantly took possession of her, like some sort of madness enveloping her—body and soul. Dakota didn't pause to think through her feelings or even acknowledge the fear that this might be a mistake. For now everything had burned away in the heat of what she was feeling.

Her lips clung to his, melting, questing.

She wasn't the kind who needed the physical aspect of lovemaking strictly for its own sake. Rather, she was the sort of woman who needed to feel something for the person she was with. Needed to believe that the man she was sharing this most intimate of moments with cared for her on some level.

Her mind would have told her no on both counts. But her soul whispered otherwise. She listened to her soul and gave herself up to the moment and the man.

Still lost in the kiss flowering through her, she was vaguely aware of stumbling backward toward the living room. Piece by piece, their clothing fell to the floor faster than leaves being stripped from a tree. The path from the kitchen to the living room was littered with them until there was nothing left between them but passion and skin.

His touch quickened her insides, making them tight. Making her anticipate. His hands seemed to be everywhere, caressing, molding, creating an inferno everywhere he touched. And everywhere he was destined to touch.

Dakota did what she could to share the experience, her hands passing over his body with searching, kneading fingertips. The very feel of his hard body heightened her excitement tenfold.

Damn it, what was he doing? Ian silently demanded of himself while he still had the strength to form a question. Was he crazy?

The answer came from somewhere within, far more serene than he felt at the moment. No. He wasn't crazy.

Kissing Dakota was the sanest thing he'd ever done. The fight against his desire to kiss her, to have her, was short-lived and fleeting.

Ian gave himself up to this sensation, to this woman who had been fashioned out of the fabric of life for this very purpose only, to complete him. To make him feel strangely whole, as if there'd been something missing all this time and he hadn't realized it until just this very moment.

Until he kissed her again.

Everything inside of him shook from the import of the revelation, even as he touched Dakota with a steady resolve and steadier hands.

Inside him nothing was steady.

His breath became short. Though in incredible shape, he felt as if he'd just run the marathon of his life. Every pulse point in his body throbbed wildly. From wanting her.

A part of him wanted to give in to the madness, to ravage her on the spot, but even in his delirium, he knew that wasn't right. It wasn't the way he wanted her to remember this. It wasn't the way he wanted to remember this.

Somehow they managed to reach the sofa, and there he pinned her down with his body. But rather than take her, rather than drive himself into her and secure the release he so desperately wanted, he refrained.

A gentleness came in the midst of the storm.

He laced his fingers through hers as he raised her hands over her head and branded her body with his lips, making her his. He kissed her neck, her shoulder, the tempting space between her breasts, working his way slowly down her body.

Dakota twisted and turned beneath him, bucking like an untamed mare. Sending the fire inside of him up more degrees than he could begin to calculate.

Arrows tipped in flame went searing through her.

Dakota could barely focus, barely stay within her head. Somewhere a distant thought told her she couldn't just let him do this to her, that she needed not only to be the recipient of lovemaking, but the provider as well.

But there was honey as well as fire inside her veins, creating a complete contradiction in terms, and there wasn't enough energy within her to push him away and weave her own spell. All she could do was absorb. Absorb and want more. Raising her body to his roaming lips, Dakota moaned his name.

The sound of her voice against his ear as he once again kissed the sensitive area along her throat inflamed him even further. Had she asked him to leap off a building for her at that moment, he would have. Would have done anything she wanted of him.

Except walk away.

Because he was her prisoner.

He knew it, and the very idea that someone had control over him to this extent shook him down to the foundation of his soul. He thought he'd lost his soul when he'd watched his ex-wife walk away with their son.

Dakota wrapped her legs around him. He could feel heat emanating from her very core. The urgent motion of her body was his complete undoing. Unable to hold back any longer, he pivoted his body over hers ever so slightly and then drove himself into her. As he did so, he felt her teeth gently catch his lower lip and suck it in.

It pushed him on.

His hips fused with hers, he began the dance that was

to become their own, moving at first slowly, then faster and faster until he brought them both up to where they desperately wanted to be.

Up to the top of the world.

She could feel stars bursting in her veins, could feel that wild rush that threatened to sweep her out into oblivion. She clung to him, wanting to prolong the sensation.

Wishing it would go on forever.

But forever had a limited life expectancy.

The descent back to the earth below, down to reality, was slow, made so because neither wanted the moment to end. Neither wanted to face the moments that came after.

They came anyway.

A coldness wedged its way into the warmth that had existed only seconds ago. Dakota tried not to notice. She struggled to catch her breath as Ian shifted his weight from her. She was afraid she would squeak if she tried to speak too soon. Stalling for time, she dragged her hand through hair that was all but plastered against her face.

Slowly, a rhythmic breathing pattern returned. She ran her tongue over her lips. "You're not going to have to put this down in your journal, are you?"

He had no idea how he managed to keep a straight face. Thoughts, emotions and, damn it, another volley of full-blooded desire rushed through him like a forest fire raging out of control.

He tucked his arm around her in the tiny space that existed between them. "Maybe under 'miscellaneous.'"

Pinned against the back of the sofa, she somehow

managed to lift up on one elbow and stare at Ian. Her eyes widened. She might have just made love with the man, but she still had little to no idea what made him tick. Each time his sense of humor surfaced, it was a surprise.

Her eyes searched his expression. "You're kidding, right?"

He wanted to kiss her again, to catch her small, perfect face in his hand and bring her mouth down to his. What was going on here? Why wasn't he getting up, walking away? Why was he lingering at the scene of a trespass that shouldn't have happened in the first place? "Yes, I'm kidding," he told her. "This is not the kind of thing you write down."

Not the kind of thing. The phrase rang in her head. How many others had he guarded, then wound up making love with? One? Two? Ten? She steeled herself off for the answer. "So you've done it before."

His eyebrows knitted together, forming a dark squiggle across which she wanted to feather her fingertips. "I have a son, Dakota. Yes, I've done it before."

Did this mean something to her? he wondered. Did all the lights suddenly go out in her world the way they had in his because the surge was too great to be handled? Where were these thoughts coming from? he demanded of himself. He never overthought a liaison before. Why now? What was it about this woman that turned his world on its ear?

She was still waiting, he realized. "No," he told her quietly, giving her more of himself than he would have wanted to under normal circumstances. But the look in her eyes forced him to be truthful. "I've never done it before with a client."

She wanted more than anything to believe him, not really knowing why it was so important to her, only that it was. But Ian was nothing if not devoted to the sanctity of his clients, to their right to privacy. "Would you tell me if you had?"

She was asking for his soul, Ian thought, without recognizing the fact that she had it. And he needed it back. But he hadn't a clue as to how to secure it again. All he knew was that he was nervous as hell.

He combed his fingers through her hair, pushing a stray lock away from her face. "Yes," he told her quietly, "I would."

Dakota wanted to feel that this night was different for him, different from all the others that had come before. Because it was different for her. She couldn't remember when her world had been rocked this way, and although the man was more than just an astute and competent lover, she knew it wasn't just because of the physical pleasure she'd experienced. Something had dislodged within her when they made love, and she was terrified.

Suddenly, right before Ian's eyes, she had turned pale. Concern nudged at him. Had he missed something? Done something wrong? Because it had all felt so right. "What's the matter?"

"Why?" She would have turned away from him if she

could, but there was nowhere to even avert her face in her present position.

He caught her face in his hand and forced her eyes to his. "Because you look as if you've just seen a ghost."

Dakota tried very hard to sound nonchalant and had no idea if she succeeded. She shrugged carelessly, acutely aware that she was completely nude, lying next to a man equally so. "Maybe the ghost of romances past."

"And?"

She blew out a breath, her eyes searching his. Looking for help. "And I don't know what to think."

"Maybe that's the problem." His voice was so low, he sounded as if he was giving voice to his own insecurities, not hers. "Maybe you shouldn't think. Maybe, just for now, just for tonight, thinking should be placed on the back burner."

And then, before she could answer, he shifted against her and, in so doing, made all the smoldering embers within her turn into bonfires again. Making love with Ian had exhausted her. But now that seemed like a hundred years ago. She was ready, willing and eager to share her body with him again. The thought slammed into her as her lips found his. What had come over her? Was she turning into some kind of a sex-starved woman?

And how could she be starved after she'd feasted so well just moments ago? There were no logical answers to her questions. All she knew was that she wanted him again, and this time, Dakota promised herself, she was going to make him just as insane as she had felt the first time.

Turning her body into his, she could feel his instant response to her. His body had hardened on first contact. A secret smile bloomed inside of her, spreading like wildfire.

"Consider it placed," she whispered, her breath caressing his face as she wove her arms around his neck and kissed him for all she was worth.

She'd sparked him. There was no question about it. Ian could feel desire closing its iron grip around him. Could feel how every point where their bodies touched aroused him again.

"This is really a first," he murmured against her mouth as he kissed her over and over again. When she drew back her head and looked at him quizzically, he realized he'd said the words out loud. He hadn't meant to. Ian searched for a way out that wouldn't give too much away. "First time with a client—"

"Pretend client," she interjected. Did that make it all right? No, it didn't. Because even as she grasped the tiny straw, she knew that her being a client wasn't what was bothering her. The problem was her reaction to him.

"And first time for other things," he finally added when she continued looking at him expectantly.

"What other things?"

He nipped at her lower lip, suckling on it as he cupped her breast, his thumb teasing her nipple. "You can't drag out all my secrets at once."

But she meant to, she thought, struggling to hang on to her mind. To herself. She was swiftly losing her hold on both. She didn't want the second time to be like the first. So, with her lips sealed to his, she surprised him by managing to turn their bodies around on the wide sofa until she was on top.

The maneuver caught Ian off guard. He stopped kissing her and looked up at the woman straddling his body. Explosions began going off in his veins. He tucked his hands around her buttocks, pressing her even closer to him.

It was all she needed to set her off and running. She drew him into her and began to move, her eyes fixed on his for as long as she could maintain the pose. Before stretching her body out along his.

She made him crazy, weaving her magic. There was no other term for it. Magic. He was a man who didn't believe in magic.

Until now.

The rest of the night was consumed in a blur of love-making and subsequent exhaustion. Somewhere along the line he managed to carry her into her bedroom. After placing her on her bed, he meant to go to his own room. But he stayed with her. And made love with her one more time.

Spent beyond measure, they fell asleep right after the last act, their bodies still entwined and strangely innocent.

The rosy hue that pulsed softly around her gave way to the sharp edges of fear as Dakota surfaced from a world of dreams and made her way back into reality.

There was a man in her bedroom, walking toward the door. He was completely nude, and even as the un-named, cloudlike cloak of fear draped itself heavily over her, she couldn't draw her eyes away from a body that was damn near perfect.

She searched for something to say. Something to make him stay without her asking. She wanted him to look at her, to tell her not to be afraid. That he was the one she was looking for. She wanted a fairy tale served on a silver tray.

Clearing her throat, she asked, "Are you sure this isn't going into the journal?" She saw him stiffen at the threshold of her room.

Damn it, she was awake. He'd hoped to be able to sneak out of the room before she opened her eyes. Served him right for not leaving the second he'd opened his.

Without turning around, he looked over his shoulder, trying not to see the way dawn had crept into the room and was now caressing her body the way he wanted to. The way he couldn't.

"I'm sure," he said gruffly, then turned away. "Go back to sleep."

Ian closed the door behind him.

The room was eerily quiet. All she heard was the sound of her own breathing.

He'd left. Just like that, she thought. No conversation, no empty words of praise. No attempt to say something about last night.

Nothing.

Because it *was* nothing, she told herself. To him. He was a man and had reacted as such, giving her what was without question the best time she'd ever had with or without her clothes on. But the fact that he didn't say something remotely friendly this morning was an obvious sign that she shouldn't make anything out of what had happened between them.

She shouldn't start hoping or taking the locks off her heart. Locks that had been there even with John, she realized. Until last night, part of her had always been held in reserve, afraid. Afraid of making a mistake. Because she'd been raised to believe with all her heart that a husband was supposed to be forever. With that thought existed the fear of making a mistake. Of giving her heart to the wrong person. Because with the wrong person a marriage would disintegrate into a divorce.

She didn't want to get divorced. She didn't want to be a statistic. What she wanted was what her parents had. A solid marriage between two people who knew they were meant for each other. Two people who were going to remain together no matter what.

The world wasn't like that anymore, a small voice echoed in her head.

Restless, she fingered the cameo around her neck. She hadn't had it off since she had bought it. Ian had come into her life the day she bought it.

Confusion nibbled at her.

She didn't believe in legends, in talismans, and yet...

She believed in happily ever after, didn't she? Damn it, why couldn't she be like other women? Why couldn't she just have a pleasurable experience and chalk it up to that? Why did it have to be serious for her?

It certainly wasn't serious for him. He didn't even stay to see if he could catch an encore this morning. Was he tired of her already? Was he one of those men who needed to prove something to himself and once that was done, he moved on?

Enough, she ordered herself. She was overthinking again. She didn't want to think at all.

Ian closed the door behind him and walked quickly to his own room. He'd had to get out of there. He'd spent the last fifteen minutes watching her sleep, aching to take her again. Not knowing what the hell had come over him. If he stayed any longer, he would have gone back to her bed. And to her.

What had he been thinking, making love with her like that? Did he think it was going to lead somewhere? Where? He was a cop for hire, a working man. And she was some kind of Hollywood royalty. Even if she wasn't, he had nothing to offer a woman. His ex had made that quite clear to him. With his way of keeping to himself and the kind of work he did, he had nothing to offer any woman.

He couldn't allow this kind of thing to happen again. And yet…

And yet nothing. He knew how to exercise control

over himself. He'd done it before. Self-discipline was a way of life with him.

He closed his own door behind him and walked into the bathroom. What he needed more than anything right now was a shower. A damn cold one. He wondered if there was a setting that would spit ice cubes at him.

Dakota hurriedly threw on her clothes and then crossed the room to her door. Cracking it open, she listened intently. She thought she detected the sound of running water. He was in the shower. Good. Now was her chance.

She edged her way out into the hall. The sound of running water was louder.

She knew she couldn't stay here, not right now. Not with all these feelings running rampant through her like pool balls after a break. She needed time to sort them out. Time to figure out what to do with this sunshine that kept popping up, followed by rain. Their lovemaking had filled her with a tremendous glow, but Ian's cavalier way of just walking out without a word all but undid her.

She needed time to put everything in its place—time without him. And there was no way she could get that unless she found a way to ditch him. He would never listen to reason and let her go off on a drive by herself. He was too stubborn, too committed to the deal he'd made with the station.

To hell with the station. To hell with him.

Dakota struggled to bank down her anger. She was her own person and she needed to find that person again.

Because somehow, amid all the lovemaking that had taken place last night, she'd gotten lost.

She tiptoed past his room, as if he could somehow hear her with all that running water. Once clear, she made a beeline for the front door. Reaching it, she felt oddly triumphant and sad at the same time.

Dakota lost no time in getting down to the parking garage and her car. Once in it, she quickly hit the street while looking in her rearview mirror for signs of Ian chasing her down.

All she saw was a navy convertible pulling out of its parking place.

Made it!

Dakota pointed her vehicle due north.

Chapter Twelve

The man in the gray sweater vest behind the counter stood about five-eight, was thin and wiry. His complexion indicated that he had spent most of his adult life indoors amid the antiques he sold and was now in the process of dusting. Upon seeing her walk in, he arrested his movement, laid down the feather duster and smiled congenially at her.

Despite the smile, Dakota noticed a sadness in his brown eyes.

"May I help you?"

Dakota looked around the small shop, but the man appeared to be alone. She felt a nibble of disappointment. "Yes, I'd like to speak to the lady who sold me this necklace, please."

The man squinted slightly at the cameo she held up for his inspection. He showed no sign of recognition, but nodded obligingly.

Turning his head, he called over his shoulder toward the storeroom in the back. "Honey, there's someone here who says she wants to speak to you." He turned to look at her again, his eyes on the necklace. "You say you bought that here?"

Dakota didn't know what to make of his uncertain expression. He obviously didn't recognize the cameo, but maybe he didn't handle the inventory.

"Yes, why?"

The man shook his head sheepishly. "It's just that I don't recognize it. But then—" he shrugged philosophically "—estate jewelry is more my wife's department."

The man's response left her a little confused since he looked to be no older than about fifty. The woman who had sold her the necklace was clearly in her mid or late seventies. Was that his wife? Could there be that much of an age gap between the two?

But then, she thought, some people aged more than others and…

The black drape that separated the storeroom from the showroom parted and a pleasant-looking woman with auburn hair and a ready smile walked out. Like her husband, she was thin and of medium height.

He beckoned her over to the counter. "Oh, Brenda, this is Ms.—"

Brenda's dark eyes all but disappeared as her smile widened. She put out both hands to take one of Dakota's.

"Dakota Delany," she finished for her husband. Leaning over the counter, the woman heartily shook her hand. "Yes, I know who you are." Beaming, she lowered her voice, as if to share a secret. "I sneak out of the showroom every day at two on the dot to watch your program on the little television set in the back. What can I do for you?"

Dakota smiled at Brenda, trying not to sound abrupt as she looked at the owner. "This isn't the woman who sold me the necklace."

Brenda's husband seemed as confused as she felt. "I'm afraid this is the only lady who works here, except for the summer when our daughter Suzie helps out." He rolled his eyes. "If you can call it that. Are you sure you didn't get this place confused with some other antique shop? There are a lot of small shops that deal in antiques in this part of the state."

Her mind felt as if it was a rumpled bed, but this was the one thing she wasn't confused about. She'd gotten the cameo here.

"No, it was here, I'm sure of it." She counted backward in her head. "I was here on Monday." Monday, the day that Ian came into her life. Which was why she was here. She wanted to talk to the woman who'd told her about the legend. Maybe she needed to speak to someone who seemed to take legends as gospel.

Right now she needed to believe in a legend.

The sad look she'd seen earlier in the man's eyes emerged again. He exchanged a brief, perplexed look with his wife.

"We were closed Monday," he told her solemnly. "My great-aunt Rachel died." He indicated the photograph behind the main counter. Its frame was draped in black velvet.

"Let me see that piece." Brenda stepped forward to take a better look at the cameo. Dakota held perfectly still, not for Brenda's perusal, but because she couldn't take her eyes off the woman in the photograph he had pointed to. Her gray hair a fluffy halo about her perfectly round face, she was smiling serenely. The woman's eyes seemed to look right into her.

She was the woman who had sold her the cameo.

Brenda had rounded the counter and was examining the cameo closely, her thin fingers lightly touching the oval. "Oh, this looks like it might have been part of the collection I just acquired from my last trip south, Josiah." She glanced at her husband. "I don't remember putting it out, but then I guess I must have." A puzzled expression came over her features again as the woman looked up at her. "And you say someone else sold you this?"

"Yes." Dakota's mouth felt very dry. They were going to think she was out of her mind, she thought. But maybe there was a relative around who looked like the owner's great-aunt. She nodded toward the photograph. "That lady."

The owner shook his head adamantly. "I'm afraid that's just not possible. My aunt Rachel was very ill the last few years of her life. Bedridden mostly. And a little out of her head," he confided. "She was almost ninety when she died." As if anticipating Dakota's next question, he added, "That photograph was taken twenty years ago."

The more she looked at the photograph, the more convinced Dakota was that it was the woman who had sold her the cameo and told her about the legend. Frustrated, knowing how this had to appear to the two people politely regarding her, she looked from the owner to his wife.

"Are you sure?"

The man opened his mouth and then closed it again, as if searching for words that weren't offensive.

"I should know the details about my own great-aunt." His tone was polite but firm. His eyes swept over the crowded space. "She used to own this store. Deeded it over to Brenda and me almost fifteen years ago because she felt she couldn't run it anymore. She helped out for a little while after that, then stopped coming in. It was very hard on her to give this up. We consulted her whenever we could just to make her feel she still had a hand in it."

The owner's wife cocked her head, peering at her. Her expression was kindly. "Are you sure you're all right?"

Dakota could have sworn she'd bought the cameo from the owner's great-aunt. But now none of it made sense anymore. "No," she murmured, feeling as if her head was in complete upheaval. "I'm not sure about anything right now." Bewildered and confused, she turned on her heel and went to the front door.

In the mirror to the right of the entrance Dakota caught a glimpse of the owners exchanging looks and shaking their heads.

"Celebrities," she heard the man mutter as a look of pity crossed his face.

Dakota closed the door behind her.

Well, that settled it. She had definitely gone over the edge. There was no other way to interpret all this. She'd bought a necklace from a woman who was probably being buried at the exact time the sale was being rung up. Then she made love with a man she hardly knew, something she never would have done.

Yet she had.

"What the hell do you think you're doing?"

Already spooked, the stern voice coming from behind her nearly made Dakota jump out of her skin. She swung around, her fist doubled, not knowing who or what to expect.

Her mouth dropped open.

Ian was the last person she'd thought she would see up here. Was he an apparition, too? A figment of her imagination? She'd left him showering in the apartment. Driving away from the city, she'd kept checking her rearview mirror for any sign of his car following her. There hadn't been any.

She saw that he had parked his car right behind hers at the leaf-littered curb. How could he have known she'd come here? She'd never given him a location, other than to say the place had been "upstate."

Damn it, she thought angrily, she was too young and too well adjusted to be having a nervous breakdown. She wanted answers.

Squaring her shoulders, she fixed him with a look. "How did you know to find me here?"

The relief that flooded through his veins when he saw her coming out of the quaint two-story, Tudor-style building had taken him by surprise. He was unaccustomed to feeling this level of concern about anyone, except his son, Scottie. Now that he'd located her, he reverted back to his old self.

An enigmatic smile moved along his lips. "Trade secret."

The hell with that, she thought. "No, no cloak-and-dagger stuff. Unless you move through walls and have some kind of long-range vision that helped you find me, I want a logical explanation."

To her surprise, his smile broadened. She liked his smile, but she still wanted answers.

"Don't get into electronics much, do you?"

Dakota crossed her arms before her chest. "Not really. What does that have to do with it?"

He took her arm, moving her away from the shop. Just in case she started shouting, he didn't want anyone overhearing her. "Let's just say I used a tracking device."

Her eyes widened as she took in the gist of his words. "You bugged me?" Opening her purse, she began rifling through it.

Very patiently Ian reached over and closed her purse before the contents started spilling out. "Not you."

"My car." It was the only logical guess left. Something about invasion of privacy hummed through her brain. Still upset about the way things had turned out between them this morning and really shaken over what the antique shop owner maintained, she took the restraints off her temper. "You bugged my car? Why?"

Taking her arm again, he guided her toward her vehicle. Dakota pulled her arm away and glared at him. "Because, after seeing you in action, I had a hunch you'd pull this kind of stunt. So I placed a tracking device on your car." He frowned at her. With everything else in shambles right now, the one thing he wanted intact was his reputation. "I said I was going to treat this like a regular assignment, and I am."

"Why would someone pay you to be their bodyguard, then try to ditch you?"

"Because they're not the one paying for the service." He thought of Harry Walters and his three teenage daughters. Keeping them safe in Cannes during the festival had been an assignment from hell. "I've been a bodyguard for the children of celebrities. Not all of them like the idea of having a shadow." He gave her a penetrating look. "But then, I don't really have to explain that to you, do I?"

His voice was cold, deliberate. Removed. It was as if they were complete strangers. As if they hadn't spent the night together.

As if it was all a figment of her imagination.

Maybe it had been. Buying the cameo from the old woman everyone swore was dead certainly looked as if it had been. But she had the cameo, damn it, Dakota thought as she fingered it. And she had seen Ian leaving her bed this morning. It was real. All of it was real.

And she still wanted answers.

Apparently, so did he. "Why did you take off like that this morning?" Ian asked.

Ever since she was a little girl, when she was at a loss for an answer, she resorted to flippancy. Nothing had changed in twenty-nine years. "They were having a sale here. I couldn't miss it. I figured I'd leave you alone. Men don't like to shop."

She could feel his eyes probing as he searched her face. "You're not a very good liar."

"Sorry." She turned away from him and went toward her car. "I'll work on it."

Instead of letting her go, he took hold of her shoulders and made her turn around to face him. When she did, he fought the very real urge to kiss her. But that would only compound the problem, not solve it.

"Look, Dakota, about last night—"

Oh no, she wasn't going to stand here while he offered up some trite excuse or, worse, said something that reeked of pity. She didn't need this.

She tried to shrug out of his hands and found that she couldn't. The hold was light, but firm. Her eyes blazed. "You don't owe me any explanations. These things happen between consenting adults. We're adults, we consented. Leave it at that."

He should have. It was for the best, he told himself. But he didn't want to leave it this way, with an awkwardness between them. Still, what could he do? Nothing had changed from this morning. She was still a celebrity darling and he was who he was, an ex-cop with alimony payments and an empty soul. She was the kind of woman who deserved something more, someone who could envelop her with love, could say the words she needed to hear. The only kind of love he would ever be able to offer was the nonverbal kind. That wouldn't be enough for someone like Dakota.

She needed someone else in her life, not him. And he needed to get back to what he was good at. Keeping people safe so they could live their lives.

He tried not to think about how he'd felt when he'd walked out of his room this morning and found that she wasn't anywhere in the apartment. In that single second when he'd realized that she'd taken off, panic gripped him. He'd never felt that before and he didn't like it. Because he was uncertain about her state of mind and because he felt he was to blame for just leaving her like that, panic's scaly fingers had torn into him, and fear had assailed him, fear that she'd gone and done something stupid.

It took him several minutes to get himself centered and back on track, back to thinking clearly. Once he was, he'd remembered the tracking device he'd attached to the underside of the rear of her vehicle. He turned it on and watched its progress on his receiver. It didn't surprise him that Dakota was on the move.

What had surprised him was that she looked to be leaving the city. Where was she going?

To her ex-fiancé?

The thought surprised him. Jealousy had never been an issue for him before. It was an issue now, and he didn't like it.

Something for him to work on, he thought.

Seeking to change the subject, for himself as well as for her, Ian nodded toward the quaint store behind her. "Did you get what you wanted?"

"No, I didn't," she murmured, thinking of the woman who wasn't there. Had the legend been part of her imagination, as well? Where did fact end and fantasy start? Damn it, she needed to know.

She was wearing a suede jacket, but it was open and he could see the cameo. Last night it was all she'd had on. He felt his body quickening at the memory and forced it away. "This the place where you got the cameo?"

Her hand covered the delicate piece, as if she was protecting it from something. "What makes you say that?"

"Looks like the kind of place that would carry something like that. Besides, you were fingering your necklace and frowning when you walked out of the shop. I thought your impulsive trip up here might have had something to do with it." When she said nothing to substantiate his deduction, he made a further guess. "Looking for matching earrings?"

It was the easy way out. If she said yes, they'd be done with it.

She didn't take it.

Maybe talking out loud with someone might put things in perspective for her, make her see something she was missing. Besides, the man had been a detective. Maybe he had an explanation for what she thought she'd seen.

"No, I came back because I wanted to talk to the woman who sold this to me. I had some…questions." Dakota refrained from elaborating. Her questions indirectly had to do with him, because he had walked into her life the very day she'd bought the cameo and put it on. And although she didn't actually believe in magic or legends, she had to admit that something had stirred within her from the first moment she'd laid eyes on Ian.

In a way it had been as if she was under some kind of spell. She supposed part of her just wanted the old woman to admit that the so-called legend was just a fabrication, a ploy to sell the cameo, nothing more. Barring that, she'd wanted to ask the woman about the original owner, to find out if Amanda's fiancé ever did return to her.

She decided it would be for the best if she didn't go on to say that the owners of the antique shop had told her she'd had a conversation with a dead woman. He'd think she was crazy and why shouldn't he? Part of her thought she was, too.

"She never finished telling me the rest of the legend," she concluded. She felt Ian studying her face. Why? Did she look like someone who'd bought jewelry from a ghost?

"And did she this time?" he asked.

"She's not there," Dakota responded evasively.

He didn't see why that would stop her. In the few days he'd spent with her, he'd come to know that the woman had the persistence of an oncoming train. "You can come back when it's not her day off."

Dakota shoved her hands into her pockets, staring off into the horizon. "I can't."

"Why?"

Dakota swung around. Her voice had a frustrated edge as she declared, "Because she's dead."

"She died right after selling you the cameo?"

Her shoulders sagged a little, like someone who saw defeat as inevitable. "No, apparently she hasn't been working in the store for a long time."

After deciding not to share this part, she had no idea why she was telling him this. He was only going to laugh at her. Or think she was a loon. But somehow the words just kept coming.

"The owner said the store was closed last Monday, which was when I bought the cameo. Closed for a funeral." She paused a moment, then said, "Hers." She searched his face for a clue as to what he was thinking. She half expected him to laugh at her, but he didn't. His restraint was admirable. "You think I'm crazy, don't you?"

To her surprise he shook his head and looked dead serious as he said, "No."

"Okay, then what?"

Because she looked so lost, he slipped his arm around her shoulders and smiled down at her face. "There are more things in heaven and earth, Horatio, than are dreamt of in your philosophy."

She blinked. "*Hamlet*? I've got a bodyguard who quotes Shakespeare?"

He debated for a moment. Ian didn't often share things, certainly not an experience that he had kept to himself for more than twenty years. But something prodded him on.

He made his decision.

"Walk with me for a minute."

Not waiting for her to respond verbally, he led the way. He took her hand in his and guided her away from the shop, away from their cars and toward the winding road that fed into the highway. The scenery was almost heart-stoppingly picturesque. Trees heavy with the multicolored leaves of autumn nodded their heads, allowing their crowns to slip and fall. Dried leaves crunched beneath their feet as they walked.

"When I was a kid," Ian began, "I had this blue bike I loved more than anything. Spent hours on it, hanging out until way after dark. My mother was always after me to come home before I got lost. One night I did get lost. I was riding around in the wooded area that ran behind the development where I lived and a fog had set in. So thick you couldn't see more than a foot in front of you. I was nine and pretty damn scared. And then, out of nowhere, I saw my uncle Danny, my dad's younger brother walking toward me. I was never so happy to see anyone in my whole life. He took my hand and told me never to do something this dumb again, then pointed me in the right direction. He walked with me a little ways. But just as I saw my house, I turned around and realized he was gone. Jumping on my bike, I pedaled like mad for home. When I got there, some of my father's friends from the precinct were there. I thought it was because they were looking for me. I told them I was okay, but that my uncle was still out there. My father—never one for interpersonal relationships—told me to shut up and go to my room. That was when my mother took me aside and told me that my uncle had just been killed in the line of duty less than an hour ago."

She stopped walking and looked at him. "But you just said—"

"Yes," he told her quietly, "I did."

Dakota caught her lower lip between her teeth. "You believe in ghosts?"

He'd never told anyone this story, not after that night. Not even his wife. There'd been no need. But it had stayed with him and whenever he felt completely alone, he remembered that night. And what may or may not have happened.

"I believe that something got me out of that area. Had I gone in the opposite direction, I would have fallen down a ravine into the river that ran along there." He sighed, then looked at her. His voice remained solemn, but his mouth curved slightly. "I guess what I'm trying to say is that you can't explain everything."

No, she thought, you can't. "Strange philosophy for a cop."

He shrugged. "I once saw someone get shot in the head with a nail from a nailgun. It was one of those freak accidents that wasn't supposed to happen. The guy lived. I saw someone else trip in the street, hit their head on the sidewalk and die." He gave her his conclusion. It was simple and complex at the same time. "Got to be something there more than we can understand." The wind was picking up. Without thinking, he lifted her collar up for her. "You ready to go back?"

She nodded. "Yes, I'm ready." She looked toward the antique shop. She knew she'd feel better if she had some confirming details. "I'd still like you to investigate this for me, though."

He followed her line of vision and smiled. "Never pegged you for a skeptic."

She returned his smile. "Never pegged you for a believer."

Ian laughed softly. "Guess we both learned something this morning."

"Guess we did."

And then he pulled on her arm, stopping her just before they reached their vehicles. When she looked at him quizzically, he framed her face and kissed her.

Honey and delight swirled through her, despite all the resolve she'd spent the morning fashioning. "What's that for?"

His eyes held hers for just a moment. "For last night."

He left the words hanging between them as he went to his car. He stood by it expectantly until she got into hers. Watching, Ian let her pull away first.

When she looked in the rearview mirror to see if he was following her, she saw that he was. And that she was smiling.

Chapter Thirteen

For two days they waltzed around each other, almost painfully polite—ever since they'd returned from the antique shop upstate. It was as if they had each decided that the only way to survive their final week together was to act as if the night of lovemaking had never happened.

Except that it had.

Ian had twice as much reason to remain as distant as he could. He'd gotten too close to her, not just on a physical level but on another plane, as well. He'd shared a story with her he'd never told anyone else. Granted, it seemed as if she needed to hear the story at the time, but still, his experience was immensely personal to him and he just didn't do personal.

Except that he had.

Maintaining mental space was twice as necessary now. But it wasn't easy. Especially since he was living in her apartment and spending every waking moment with her. He was looking forward to the end of this experiment come Monday. And strangely dreading it at the same time.

His life couldn't be called complacent, but there had been a routine—a routine that was being badly altered by this live wire he had sworn to protect. He was beginning to have grave doubts that his life would ever get back to normal once this was over.

So when Dakota waved an invitation in front of him less than ten minutes after they'd arrived home from the studio, he found his patience in short supply. Catching her hand, he held it still long enough to read the words embossed on the ivory rectangle.

Reading didn't bring pleasure.

He raised an eyebrow and looked at her over the elaborate script. "A fund-raiser, huh?"

Taking back the invitation, which was a mere formality in her case, she smiled. "Yes."

"And you have to go." He didn't bother suppressing his sigh.

Dakota dropped the invitation on the VCR within her entertainment unit. "I already RSVP'd that I was coming." And had been quickly commandeered to step in as acting cochairperson since one cochairperson had come down with a raging case of the flu. At the time she'd received the invitation, the "and guest" embossed on it had meant John. Now, however, it was going to mean her bodyguard. She looked at him, humor playing along the curve of her lips. "But you don't have to."

Didn't she ever get tired of playing that same old tune? She knew damn well what the terms of their agreement were. "Yes, I do," he responded reluctantly.

She cocked her head, studying him. Trying not to get sidetracked by the hard, chiseled planes and angles of his face and the way they made her pulse accelerate. "Not that you ever sounded eager about anything, but I sense a really huge display of foot-dragging here. Why?"

He didn't see the point in denying how he felt. Formal affairs were a huge pain in the seat, literally and otherwise. "I hate monkey suits."

"Then we won't mug a monkey and make you wear one," she quipped. Still studying him, she took measure of his frame. He hadn't been away from her to go to a gym, but she knew for a fact that one didn't get a body like that by having UPS deliver it. "What are you, a size forty-four long?"

The accuracy of her guess caught him off guard. "How did you know?"

Dakota grinned. "I've got an eye for that kind of thing." Crossing to the coffee table, she reached for the cordless phone. "I can have Olaf send over a tux for you. Or you could go down and try one on first if you like."

He stopped her from pressing the buttons on the keypad and, his hand over hers, he pushed the receiver back onto the cradle. "Olaf?"

She could always call the man later. Forty-four long wasn't that unusual, and Olaf had various friends in the business. They'd come up with a tux for Ian.

She nodded in response to Ian's query. "He used to be my father's personal tailor until he decided to come back to his roots and open up a shop in New York. My grandfather lent him seed money. I send him business whenever I can. He's really very good."

Her endorsement didn't change how he felt about wearing something so confining. "I don't care how good this Olaf guy is, it's still a monkey suit."

"No," she corrected patiently, already envisioning Ian in one, "it's a tux, and I have a feeling that you'll look very good in it."

Ian could see his fate—and doom—in her eyes.

Very good was an understatement, Dakota thought the following evening as she gave Ian the once-over in the living room. The man looked downright gorgeous in the tuxedo that Olaf had sent. Always thinking one step ahead, Olaf had sent along his personal assistant for any last-minute alterations. None were necessary. Ian was a perfect forty-four long.

The back of his black hair brushed ever so lightly against his collar as she walked around him, carefully surveying him from every angle. He didn't have a bad side. But then, she already knew as much.

Dakota felt her palms itch and pressed them against her thighs. "You clean up very well, Ian Russell."

Turning his head, he glanced at her. "Ditto." He felt like some kind of mannequin on display at Saks Fifth Avenue.

Finished with her tour, Dakota came to a stop where she had begun. Directly in front of him. She grinned at his response. "Ditto. Now there's a line to turn any woman's head."

Oddly self-conscious, Ian shrugged. "You know what I mean."

She cocked her head, regarding him for a moment longer before she said, "Yes, I suppose I do. Would be nice to hear the words, though."

"I'm not any good with words."

She blew out a disparaging breath. "Even that monkey you were identifying with can be trained to learn if it wants to."

"I wasn't identifying with any monkey. I called this a monkey suit," he corrected.

She appeared unfazed by his need for accuracy. "Whatever." Her eyes slid along his form one last time. "Ready to go?"

He was ready to stay right where he was. For more reasons than one. Dakota looked mouthwateringly beautiful in her red floor-length gown. The slit on the left ran almost all the way up her thigh, making him want to take the same path with his hand and explore it all over again. The fabric clung to her every breath and even now he could feel his body tightening with desire as he struggled to blank out his mind. With the way he felt, he knew his safest bet was to be out in the open with her, preferably in a crowd scene. Like the fund-raiser.

He nodded in answer to her question. "Yeah, I'm ready."

She began to walk to the door, but glanced at him over her shoulder. "Smile. You look like a man whose shoes are pinching him too tightly."

"It's not my shoes," he said. After draping the black velvet cape she'd handed him around her shoulders, he opened the front door for her.

Dakota smiled to herself as she walked out of the apartment.

Ian cooled his heels at the bar, nursing the same drink he'd held in his hand for the last hour. And all the time he'd watched her work the room like a pro. It seemed as if no one could say no to the woman. He took another perfunctory sip of his scotch and soda.

Dakota had failed to tell him that she was cochairwoman of the fund-raiser and, as such, she took it upon herself to loosen every person's grip on their wallet or purse strings. As she wove her way from table to table, smiling, pausing to chat, he found himself thinking that the process appeared to be almost a painless one for the donors. Not everyone looked as if they'd been preserved in ice for the last fifty years.

Jealousy pricked at him as he observed the way some of the men looked at her. As if she was the last club sandwich on a tray, and they were going off an eight-day fast.

A host of unprofessional reactions assaulted him. Annoyed with himself, Ian knew he had to get a grip. But it wasn't easy, not when he was watching her move so seductively from group to group, her hips swaying ever so invitingly.

He took another sip, finally finishing his drink. And wanting more.

Dakota smiled to herself as she jotted down the latest name and pledge amount on the small ledger she carried with her. Relying on mutual connections, first-hand encounters and previous relationships, she had managed to charm her way into getting almost a hundred thousand dollars in pledges.

Not bad for an evening's work, she thought. And the evening was still young.

A familiar tune drifted through the air. It took her a second to realize that the band had begun playing, now that dinner was over. She closed her eyes for a moment and let the melody seep into her. Her hips swayed a little in time to the music.

"Would you like to dance?"

She could have sworn that the voice belonged to Ian, but she had to be imagining things. Ian wasn't the type of man to ask a woman to dance. He was the type to beg off, mumbling something about having two left feet or a phobia of being on a crowded dance floor. Or maybe an old injury, sustained in the line of duty, that only flared up if his feet had to move in time to the music.

Turning around, she saw that he was standing right there behind her.

She tucked her ledger back into the small purse she'd brought and shook her head, as if to clear it. "I'm sorry, did you say something?"

"I asked you if you'd like to dance," Ian repeated. Was it the scotch? She looked even more beautiful now than when they'd first walked in.

"I'd love to dance." Humor curved her mouth as she pretended to look around. "You have anyone in mind?"

His brows narrowed, and he moved in a step closer. "Well, since the question came from me, I figured—me."

"You dance." The words were half a statement, half a question uttered in disbelief.

"I wouldn't be asking you to dance if I didn't." He took her hand in his and led her to the dance floor. "What's so funny?"

"Nothing." More easily than she thought possible, she slipped her hand into his and began to dance. "I just can't picture you wanting to learn how to dance."

He was good, she thought. Very good. But then, pride probably kept him from being anything less than good, no matter what he undertook.

"Wanting had nothing to do with it." He placed his hand at the small of her back, coming in contact with bare skin. It seemed as if her dress was being held up by magic and possibly crazy glue. "My mother told me she figured I needed social graces."

She tilted her head to look up at him. "Wise woman, your mother."

He shrugged carelessly. "Not so wise, she married my father."

A world of questions popped into her head. For now, she banked them down. If she started asking, she knew he'd clam up and this moment would be gone.

"If she hadn't, there wouldn't have been you." She turned her face up to his. "I'm a firm believer in destiny. How about you?"

When she leaned her head back like that, he could feel her hair brushing up along the back of his hand. The sensation sent tiny shock waves through him. "I believe in the moment."

She regarded him with amusement. "As in living in it?"

"Yes."

She nodded. "That's good, too." The music pulsed through both of them and they moved with it as if they were two halves of a whole. Excitement snaked through her like an electric eel, sending off sparks in its wake. "Did your mother teach you how to dance?"

"Yes."

Dakota caught her lower lip between her teeth as she regarded him. "Did she teach you any other social graces?"

He thought a moment, or pretended to. "To keep my mouth shut when I couldn't say something nice."

She thought of his close-mouthed persona. If she didn't prod him, she had no doubt that he would have perhaps let only a dozen sentences fall, all centering around her lax approach to personal security. "And you took that to the nth degree, right?"

His eyes held hers for a long moment, and she would have sold her soul to know what he was thinking. "Like I said—"

"You're not good with words," she concluded for him. "Yes, I know, we've already had this conversation." Her eyes searched his, looking for clues, for something she couldn't put a name to. Or was afraid to. "I was hoping for a different outcome this time."

"Why?" he asked. "Don't you have enough people telling you that you're beautiful? That looking at you makes a man weak in the gut and that all he can think of is making love with you?"

"Never enough," she breathed, her heart having lodged in her throat. Excitement raced through her.

"Well," he began, turning her so they pivoted sharply. She felt his hand press against her back. Thrilling her. "You won't hear it from me no matter how true it is."

"Okay." Leaning her cheek against his shoulder, she breathed in the light scent of his cologne and let herself be taken away.

Ian felt the warmth of her breath even through his tuxedo jacket. Felt, too, the call of desire. His hand pressed her closer to him, almost as if it had a mind of its own.

Just like the rest of his body.

Humming, Dakota sailed into the foyer through the door that he had unlocked for her. "God, it was a wonderful night," she declared.

The hour was late. The party had lasted until two o'clock in the morning, and she had stayed to the very end, coaxing, cajoling and adding to the pot by another thirty thousand dollars. It was only a drop in the bucket as far as research for Parkinson's was concerned. But it helped. Every little bit helped, she told herself.

She was flying, she realized, and she didn't want to come in for a landing.

He watched Dakota weave ever so slightly as she dropped the shoes she was carrying on the floor. She looked particularly small to him. Small and delicate. And delectable. He felt large and clumsy in contrast. Like a bear standing beside a porcelain angel.

To his surprise, instead of heading for her bedroom, Dakota pivoted on her heel and began to push his jacket from his shoulders.

"Olaf wants his merchandise back now?" he queried. He tried to temper the heat he was feeling with amusement. But all he could think of was making love with her again.

After tugging the garment from his arms, she tossed it over the back of the sofa. "I want to see what it looks like back in the box."

He laughed, staying her hands as her fingers reached for his shirt. "I think you had a little too much to drink."

She pretended to be indignant at the implication. "I had only two glasses. Besides, my intoxicated state has nothing to do with alcohol." She sniffed. Then a huge grin broke out with the ease of sunrise. "Larry told me that he'd never raised as much money for The Parkinson's Foundation as we did tonight."

"As *you* did tonight," he corrected. Whoever this Larry person was, from what he could see, the man had been content to stand back and let Dakota do the bulk of the work.

Beaming, Dakota paused in her assault on him to take a little bow. "I guess I did have something to do with it." Her eyes shone with mischief as she looked at him. "Hey, don't change the subject, we were talking about seeing the tux back in the box."

"No, we weren't." He took a step back from her. If she kept this up, he wasn't going to be responsible for his reaction. "But if that's what you want, give me a second to change."

But as he began to leave the room, she caught hold of the bottom of his shirt, pulling it out of the cummerbund. Tugging, she managed to stop him in his tracks. "Where are you going?"

He nodded in the direction of his bedroom. "I thought—"

Maybe her little bit of champagne had gone to her head, but she doubted it. She'd been able to consume much more than that and not feel its effects. No, this was something more. This was euphoria coupled with the very real knowledge that their time together was finite. And she'd made up her mind to make the most of what she had in front of her. Sans consequences, sans regrets.

"No, don't think." It was a request, not an order. "Just for tonight—"

"This morning—" he corrected.

"See, you're still doing it." She framed his face with her hands and stood up on her toes. "No thinking," she urged. "Just feeling."

Any hopes of withdrawing, if they had truly existed, faded from view. Ian slipped his arm around her waist, pulling her closer. "What if I don't want to feel what I'm feeling?"

"And what is it you're feeling?" Her voice was soft, seductive. His pulse scrambled.

He couldn't get himself to look away from her eyes. Couldn't get himself to do the right thing and leave. Nothing existed beyond this room. Beyond her. But on some level he knew that there was a minefield to cross.

"That if I'm not careful, I'm going to make another mistake."

She tilted her head ever so slightly, her eyes still on his. "Sure it's a mistake?"

"I'm sure." It was a mistake to let himself be drawn out, a mistake to allow any of his feelings to surface. Nothing could come of these moments they spent together, as much as he wanted them to continue. Already he'd stopped being his own man. He wanted to be hers.

"Are you going to make it, anyway?"

He cupped her cheek, then slowly drew a lock of her hair away from her face, tucking it behind her ear. "Looks like."

Dakota shook the lock free, letting it fall into her face again. Very carefully, she drew a few pins out, letting the rest of her hair fall around her shoulders. She looked like a blond gypsy.

Smiling up into his face, she brushed her lips against his. "Good. I thought I was going to have to use your gun on you."

"My gun?" To his surprise, she stepped back, her eyes laughing at him. In her hand she had the service revolver that he thought was still holstered at the small of his back. As if to assure himself that she had it, he felt the space. Nothing but an empty holster met his touch. "How did you—?"

"I learned a lot of tricks growing up on movie lots," she told him. Stunt people and doubles were always showing her how to do things that she wouldn't have ever been able to place on her résumé. "Don't worry." Very gingerly, she handed the weapon to him butt first. "The safety's still on."

Stripping off his holster, Ian placed it and the weapon on the coffee table. "I wish I could say that about us."

"You want to be safe?" Again she searched his face, seriously this time, for some sign that she could work with.

Ian moved his head slowly from side to side, his eyes never leaving hers. "No."

Her smile returned, taking possession of all of her this time. "Me, neither."

He couldn't resist any longer. He'd wanted to kiss her, to hold her and run his hands along her body, canceling out the possessive glances all the other men had been giving her all evening.

With hurried hands, Dakota began working the buttons on his shirt, pulling them out of their holes, tugging the rest of the shirt out.

"Hey, hold it," he chided, stopping her hands before she could tear something. The tuxedo was scheduled to go back to her friend later that morning. "Aren't you afraid you might rip it?"

That was the last thing on her mind. "I'll pay for anything I damage," she promised.

He wondered if that included something a lot less tangible than a custom-made shirt. But there already was damage to the insulating wall he'd kept around himself. And he was the one who was going to have to pay for that, not her. Tomorrow or the next day or the end of the week.

But all of that seemed so far away right now, and she was so close.

As close as his desire for her.

Passions he'd held in check all evening, all day, exploded. Executing sure, true movements, he had Dakota out of her gown before she could finish undressing him. She stood before him in stockings, heels and a thong that exposed more than it hid. He thought he was going to swallow his tongue.

His eyes seemed to devour her, and she felt her body heating. "If I'd gone like this, I could have doubled the donations," she speculated, her voice husky.

"You wouldn't have gone like this," he said, his fingers tangling in the silken scrap that served as underwear.

She shivered as he worked the tiny bit of material down the length of her thighs. Dakota stepped out of it, kicking the thong aside. "Why?"

He grasped her buttocks, pressing her against him. Against the desire that ran full-blooded through him. "Because I wouldn't have let you."

Since the day she'd first opened her eyes, she'd never doubted she was an independent woman with a mind of her own. So why wasn't she balking at this display of male possessiveness? Why was her heart racing this way?

Because he wanted her. And she wanted to be wanted.

Chapter Fourteen

In the next moment all logic evaporated completely, sizzled into nothingness by the heat Ian generated just by touching her. By kissing her. And by the promise of what she knew was to come.

He was making her go limp even as everything within her tightened in anticipation.

With urgent fingers, she forced herself to pull off the rest of his clothing before her energy vanished. She sent them flying out of the way.

Dakota desperately wanted to run her palms along his hard, taut body, wanted the thrill that touching him evoked within her. A hunger gnawed at her belly to the point that she hardly recognized herself.

It didn't matter. Nothing mattered but this moment. And him.

This was no less a mistake the second time around than it had been the first, and yet Ian didn't care. If anything, he had even less willpower to resist her now than he did then.

This lack of restraint would have worried him had he been able to think clearly. Or at all. But what governed every ounce of his being now was the desire to have her again. To make love with her as many times as was humanly possible and then, if there was an ounce of mercy in the universe, to expire with her in his arms.

This connection couldn't go anywhere. But it didn't matter. Later it would. But now was all there was.

Pushing her down to the floor where she was cradled in a makeshift comforter made up of their tangled, discarded clothing, Ian sought to ignite every inch of her skin by deftly passing his hands, his lips and his tongue over her twisting body.

The sound of her breathing, growing audible and shorter, had the blood within his veins accelerating faster than he thought possible. Her belly quivered as he stroked the taut area with his tongue, working his way lower. Anticipation and desire urged him on.

Dakota grabbed fistfuls of the clothing beneath her as she scrambled inwardly toward the pulsating excitement. The climax came from nowhere, exploding, lighting up her world. Leaving her tottering on the brink of exhaustion.

And then he began again.

Gasping for air, she somehow managed to pull herself up on elbows that were the consistency of spaghetti. With what very probably was her last ounce of strength, Dakota pushed him down to the rug and reversed their positions.

"What are you up to?" His voice was husky. Thrilling as it rippled along her skin.

Mischief curved her mouth. "Watch and see." She began to return the favor by initiating the exquisite torture. Anointing his body with her lips and tongue, she heightened both their anticipation and excitement.

He felt himself coming to the point of no return. He gripped her shoulders and drew her up until her body covered him and her face loomed over his. There was confusion in her eyes.

"Together," was all he said.

She understood. Parting her legs, she made the invitation clear.

And then he was there, inside her, moving so that the exhilaration built between them. The sensations immediately began to climb, to escalate, as they swiftly approached the highest summit.

She cried out his name as she reached it.

Dakota sat before her dressing table, staring at the various, carefully lined-up little jars, not seeing them at all. Seeing instead the inside of sadness. The emotion was large and empty and threatened to swallow her up whole.

She struggled to keep out of its reach without knowing if she was destined to win or lose.

After the night of the fund-raiser, their evenings had fallen together naturally. She and Ian silently stopped pretending that they could just walk away from the lovemaking. They couldn't. Every night was a celebration. And in the wee hours after that, they talked. He even told her about his son, about how much he missed Scottie, missed being with him.

"Then do something about it," she'd counseled.

"I can't. He's on the West Coast. In San Francisco."

"Last I checked, they had planes that went there. Telephone wires that hook up there. E-mail."

But he'd shaken his head. "My ex said she didn't want me in the picture, that it would only confuse him."

"What will confuse him is that the dad he loves doesn't want to have anything to do with him," she'd said. "Kids are like flowers with sunshine—they need lots of it. Find a way to get in contact with him. Neither one of you will regret it."

He'd held her tighter and she'd felt for the first time that she was really a part of his life.

The rest of the time, Dakota felt as if she was playacting, engaged in some vast charade, pretending that their nights together didn't leave an imprint on her heart.

She sighed as she picked up a makeup brush. She was in love with the man.

In her soul she knew that it wasn't a by-product of his being her bodyguard because, outside of the incident at the nightclub, Ian wasn't really her protector at all.

He was the other half of her soul.

The problem was Ian didn't know it. Had made no indication that once he was on the show again today and the "noble experiment" was over, that he wanted to remain in her life. He didn't talk about the future, didn't talk about anything but the moment.

That should have been enough, but it wasn't.

Picking up a tube of lipstick from the tray, Dakota forced herself to apply it. She had to get ready. It was almost time to go on.

Funny, she'd thought living in the moment was what she wanted. But she'd lied to herself. What she wanted was the future on a silver platter. What she wanted was what her parents had. Forever. And a family.

Boy, she could sure pick 'em, she thought, putting the tube back down. Here she was, placing her hopes and dreams on a man who was all set to vanish into the night like smoke. She'd given Ian every indication this last week that she was willing to continue if that was what he wanted. Every indication that was nonverbal. Because he wasn't the type of man to talk about feelings, and she wanted to respect that…even as she mentally threw darts at the concept.

She looked for her eyebrow pencil and sent things scattering as she foraged. Damn it, she wanted words, wanted to hear him say "I love you," "I want you" just once.

Finding the pencil, she glared at it.

Okay, not just once, maybe a few times. Like every other week and twice on holidays.

She sighed, shaking her head as she twirled the unused eyebrow pencil in her fingers. She stared at the reflection in her mirror. A less-than-happy woman stared back at her.

Because, as of today, it was over. As of today, she was once again a liberated woman, free to come and go whenever and wherever she pleased without a shadow dogging her every movement. As of this afternoon, right after the show, she wouldn't have a bodyguard in her life.

Wouldn't have *him* in her life.

The thought was killing her, and there wasn't a damn thing she could do about it, because she wasn't going to beg, wasn't going to ask. *Something* had to come from him. Ian Russell was an alpha male, for heaven's sake. He knew how to make the next move.

So why didn't he?

The answer was painfully clear. Because he didn't want to.

Looking into the mirror again, she saw a sheen covering her eyes. Terrific, five minutes before airtime and she was going to cry.

Banishing the disgust from her face, she braced her hands on the vanity table and took in several deep breaths, blowing each one out slowly. Trying to cleanse her mind and her soul.

It wasn't working.

"Aren't you supposed to be pregnant before you start

practicing Lamaze techniques?" MacKenzie quipped, peering into the dressing room. She let herself in and then stopped dead. Huge green eyes turned on Dakota as if seeing her for the first time. "Oh, my God, you're not—" She swallowed, unable to force the word out. She looked as if she was going to hyperventilate. "Are you?"

"No!" Dakota declared emphatically. "I am not pregnant."

MacKenzie scrutinized her face. "But you are sleeping with him."

Dakota avoided looking at her best friend's eyes. She hadn't told even MacKenzie that she was.

MacKenzie had a way of seeing into her, which was not always welcome. "What makes you say that?"

So that Dakota was forced to look at her, MacKenzie rested her posterior against the vanity table. "I'm your best friend, Dakota, and I've known you for a very long time. You have that look on your face. That look that says you think you're headed for trouble. Being a vastly self-assured and immensely competent woman, that only happens when you're sleeping with someone." No longer searching Dakota's face, she had her answer. "You overthink relationships, you know."

Dakota blew out an impatient breath. "There is no relationship."

"Then you're not sleeping with him?" The tone of MacKenzie's voice said she thought otherwise.

Dakota opened her mouth, then shut it again. "There is no relationship," she repeated, pushing away from the table. This, she thought as she regarded her reflection, was as good as it was going to get today.

"Sex with no commitment," MacKenzie said. "Welcome to my world." She tried to offer condolences, but the effort fell short of being convincing. "I'd say I'm sorry, but he *is* beautiful. Better to sample paradise and walk away than never to have sampled it at all."

That sounded like something that had been stuffed into a fortune cookie. "Is that supposed to make me feel better?"

Rising to her toes, MacKenzie kissed her cheek and then patted her shoulder. "No, that's supposed to get you in gear for the show. You're on in a minute and you have to say goodbye to him on the air." She paused, realizing how somber that sounded. "At least goodbye to him as your bodyguard."

She knew MacKenzie was trying to spare her feelings. *Too late.* "It'll be an all-round goodbye."

On her way out, MacKenzie paused to straighten the cameo that had twisted slightly on its black velvet ribbon. Her smile was encouraging. "Who knows? You can never tell about these things."

Dakota was tempted to rip off the cameo. Had she not been wearing it, had she never gone to that quaint little shop with its supposedly ethereal saleswoman, she wouldn't have been unconsciously predisposed toward finding someone. Wouldn't have let herself believe that things like true love still happened.

But as her hand covered the small oval, Dakota relented and then dropped her hand to her side. There was no point in yanking the cameo off. It was just a lovely piece of jewelry, a keepsake, nothing more. She'd just gone temporarily insane for a while, that was all. But she was better now.

"I can," she informed MacKenzie just before she walked past her. Trying not to think about anything but her cues, Dakota hurried down the corridor to the soundstage.

Ian was waiting in the wings, looking uncomfortable, just as he had the first day.

Good, she thought. Squirm a little.

But even as the thought emerged, she banished it. There was no point in being angry at him. Ian couldn't help being what he was any more than she could help being what she was. A dreamer. A dreamer in love with a man who didn't dream.

Coming up to him, she forced an easy, impersonal smile to her face. "Ready?"

Ian was ready to leave, to throw caution to the winds and just run off with her. But that would be stupid. And she would live to regret it, forcing him to feel the same.

So he took a deep breath, then nodded, keeping his mind on the show. "I guess."

With a quick nod of her head, Dakota sailed out onto the set, her audience face in place. Applause swelled as she sat down on the sofa where she conducted her interviews.

"Well, ladies and gentlemen, the day's finally here. The experiment is over, and after the show, I'm going to be officially bodyguardless." She rolled her eyes for their benefit. "It has been a very long two weeks."

But not nearly long enough, a voice in her head echoed.

"Bring him out, bring him out." A chant swelled until it included most of the audience.

Dakota held up her hands to quiet them. "Never let it be said that I don't listen to my audiences." Did her laugh sound as forced as she thought it did? Going through the motions, she beckoned to the wings. "Send the man out, MacKenzie. Settle down now," she ordered playfully as several women yelled out encouragements to Ian.

She waited until he was seated and the noise had died down again.

"So, tell me, what's next for you, now that you don't have to be guarding my body anymore?" she asked.

Instead of answering right away, Ian attempted to get comfortable on the sofa. He crossed his ankle over his knee and tried to focus on her question and not on the fact that she was no longer going to be part of his everyday life. He was supposed to feel relieved that it was over, not annoyed.

And certainly not grappling with this sadness that kept surfacing.

"Well, we—the firm," he quickly clarified, "have been getting a lot of calls requesting our services—" According to Randy, they were booked solid for the next nine months.

"I'll bet!" someone in the audience shouted.

"Behave," Dakota chided playfully. She felt anything but playful, but her acting genes refused to show what she was really feeling. "Go on," she urged Ian.

Leaning forward, he tried not to notice the way the light was hitting her face. Tried not to notice that the twisting feeling in his gut was all but cutting off his air supply…and that he was miserable.

"There's too much work for just the two of us anymore. Randy's already taken on a few employees and we might have to hire more."

It sounded as if he really was going to be busy for the next few months. Which left her out of the picture. No matter how she approached it, she couldn't find a way to make peace with the concept. Except that she knew she had to.

"Well, glad we could help beef up your clientele," she responded glibly.

Randy, held in check by typical New York gridlock, finally made it to the studio and joined them for the last fifteen minutes of the segment.

The segment ran over, but not as long as the last time. Going to commercial, she nodded genially at the two men as the director led them off the stage. Several women in the audience vocalized their disappointment.

Get in line, she thought, keeping her sunny smile in place. She congratulated herself on pulling the segment off without breaking. She didn't want anyone knowing just how personal the relationship between her and Ian had gotten, least of all, Ian. If he was going to handle this as if it had all been business as usual, well, damn it, so could she.

Besides, it was her fault for letting herself get carried away, not his.

She felt as if this had been the longest show of her career, but finally it was over. Waving at the audience, Dakota withdrew. There was no way she was going to face another question-and-answer period. Not today.

As she walked off the set, she saw Ian coming out of the producer's office. He was pocketing an envelope. Randy was nowhere in sight.

Ian looked right at her, killing any hope of making a quick, unobserved getaway. So she approached him. "I thought he already paid you."

His tongue felt as if it was tying itself in a knot in his mouth. Ian tapped his inside pocket. "This was a bonus."

Her eyebrows drew together. She didn't remember hearing anything about a bonus. Did Alan think she was that hard to work with?

"For what?" she asked. "For putting up with me?"

The shrug was careless, noncommittal. He'd turned down the extra money, but Randy had said it could go toward expanding the firm. He deferred to Randy's judgment. "The show's ratings were the highest you've had all year. He just wanted to show his gratitude."

"How honest of him."

God, that sounded so stilted, she upbraided herself. Why did she feel so awkward with a man she'd made love with? Why couldn't she be a love-'em-and-leave-'em type? Men fantasized about women like that. They didn't fantasize about women who wanted to be domestic or at least partially domestic. She needed to not put her heart into the mix when she dated.

But that wasn't her style.

Frustrated, at a loss for words for possibly the first time in her life, Dakota sank her hands into her pockets. There was nothing left to do but tie up the ends. "Well, I guess we'd better get back to my place so you can pack your things."

He shook his head, giving no indication that he was going anywhere. "There's no need. I already packed everything."

"When?"

Confusion worked its way through her. They had made love last night until the wee hours of today and then they'd fallen asleep in her bed. Granted, he wasn't there when she woke up this morning, but the strong aroma of coffee coming from the kitchen had told her that he'd left her side to make it for her. Just the way she liked it. As black as pitch and twice as strong.

"Early this morning."

Something twisted in her heart. He couldn't wait to make his getaway, she thought. All right, if that was the way it was going to be, she could handle it. She'd survived worse things.

She started to head toward her dressing room to get her purse. "I guess we'll go and pick it up, then."

"No need." His words stopped her in her tracks. "My suitcase is already in my car."

He was trying to break all ties with her as quickly as possible. Why wasn't she attempting to save face by walking away? Why was she just standing here, making offers that were being rejected even as he was rejecting her?

She caught her lower lip between her teeth, then asked, "Would you like a lift?" As usual, they'd driven over to the studio in her car this morning. The trip had been mostly in silence.

"Randy's going to take me over to your parking garage. He's talking to MacKenzie right now," he added.

He had an answer for everything, Dakota thought. It was time to pick up her marbles and go home.

"Okay, then I guess there's nothing left to do but say goodbye." Forcing a smile to her lips, she put out her hand to him.

It was better this way, he told himself. Better for her. Because she deserved someone who could give her what she needed. He couldn't. He'd failed at marriage, and she wanted happily ever after, something he obviously couldn't do. She wanted words, and he was inarticulate. That wasn't remotely compatible. Better to go now and not compound the mistakes he'd already allowed himself to commit.

Nodding, Ian took the hand she offered and shook it. "Guess not. Goodbye."

The smile on her lips lasted only long enough for her

to release his hand and turn away from him. With hurried steps she managed to duck into her dressing room before the tears that stung her eyes had a chance to materialize and completely humiliate her.

In the distance she heard his heels against the tile, walking away from her.

Chapter Fifteen

It wasn't changing. Wasn't lessening, wasn't getting even the smallest bit better. The sadness refused to go away.

The apartment still felt like an empty cavern to her. When she'd broken up with John, after her initial anger and hurt had a chance to settle down, a wave of relief had followed. The kind of relief that came when a big mistake had been averted at the eleventh hour.

In her heart she knew that John wasn't the man she wanted to spend forever with. Even when she'd said yes to him, there had been that tiniest bit of doubt in the back of her mind, that desire to pull back and hold fast to "no." She'd just thought she was getting cold feet way ahead of schedule, but it had turned out to be a premonition. Ultimately he hadn't been the one for her.

It was different now.

The curtain had gone down on her and Ian, but the relief she expected to finally materialize refused to come. The sadness that had been her companion waking and sleeping refused to let relief even sit at the table.

So, she threw herself into things, made sure she was as busy as any three human beings could possibly be. By the time she crossed the threshold to her darkened apartment each evening, she was several steps beyond exhausted.

But even so, every night, before she took off her coat or even shed her shoes, she instantly went to the answering machine. When the light blinked seductively at her, her heart would jump and a prayer would explode in her brain as she hoped against hope that Ian had finally called.

Night after night it was the same thing.

His voice wasn't on the machine.

Her grandfather, serving as an emcee for an award program that was being televised both in L.A. and New York, dropped by for a visit the third week into her Ian-free life. She greeted the older man's presence with the joy she always did.

And couldn't help thinking that Ian would have liked to meet him.

Everything brought back thoughts of Ian to her. One would have thought she'd spent a lifetime with him instead of only two weeks. Somehow two weeks were enough.

And not nearly enough.

"If you frown like that, your face'll freeze, Baby Cakes," Waylon Montgomery had said to her, using the nickname he'd given her at the age of four when cupcakes had been her food of choice. "Who's the guy?"

She'd insisted that her grandfather stay at her apartment, the way he always did when he came to town. They'd been getting ready for the Award Program at the time he'd sprung his question. She'd looked at him innocently. "What guy?"

He'd raised her chin with the crook of his finger. "Can't fool a fooler, Baby Cakes. Your mama had the same look in her eyes when she fell for your dad. Who is he and do I need to have a talk with him?"

"Nobody you know and no, you don't. He's out of my life."

He'd eyed her and she'd turned away, afraid he would see the sadness in her soul. "By choice?"

"Yes."

He let her finish fixing his tie. It had been her official job since she was eight. "Well, if that's the case, then he's an idiot and you're better off without him."

She only wished she'd believe that.

Her grandfather came and went. And the sadness continued, burrowing in deeper by the day. She began to think of it as a way of life. Forcing a smile to her face when she faced her friends and the audience was more and more difficult.

"Damn it," she said now to the reflection in the mirror as she wiped away a smudge she'd created with her eyeshadow wand, "It's been over a month. He's not coming back, not calling. Grow up, already."

She heard the door behind her opening and glanced up, a dismissal on her lips. The only one who walked in unannounced like that was MacKenzie. They were close enough for her friend to endure the moods she showed no one else.

"Go away, I'm trying to get my audience mood in gear, and it's not working." By her watch, she had ten minutes to get rid of the foul mood and become her former perky self.

"I thought that came naturally to you."

The brush she was about to apply to her cheeks slipped from her suddenly lax fingers, clattering to the table before rolling off and onto the floor.

Dakota swung around on her chair, certain that she was hallucinating. After all, the man's presence persistently littered her dreams every single night and twice on Sundays.

He was there, in the doorway, larger than life and three times as good-looking. The air in the dressing room became dangerously thin. She couldn't take her eyes off him. He wasn't fading, wasn't disappearing.

"Ian?"

He eased the door closed behind him. Like a man standing in the middle of a field filled with land mines, he debated the wisdom of taking a step. "You say that as if you expect me to rip a mask off my face and become someone else."

Dakota realized that she had to remind herself to breathe. She struggled to keep from flinging herself into his arms. On the flip side, that same restraint kept her from giving in to the impulse of strangling him with her bare hands.

"Maybe," she allowed tentatively. She pressed her lips together to keep any unauthorized squeals from escaping. He was here, he was really here, standing in her dressing room.

Why?

She forced the question to her lips. "What are you doing here? Did you forget something?"

He felt awkward, like a fish that found it had feet and could walk on land. It still didn't make it easy. "Yeah, I did."

Same old Ian, she thought. Getting something out of him was like pulling teeth. She was prepared to extract every one in his mouth if she had to. He'd come to her, not she to him. "What?"

"How to take a chance."

An impatient sigh didn't escape her lips, she pushed it out. "I'm sorry, but I don't understand."

That made two of them. He hadn't been able to understand anything since the day he'd walked into her apartment, least of all himself.

"Neither do I, really," he admitted. Ian looked at the padded chair on the side. "Mind if I sit down?"

Yes, I mind. I mind you coming in here after an entire silent, awful month, acting as if nothing ever hap-

*pened between us, as if my heart hasn't been cracking
and breaking the whole time. Damn it, how could you
have walked out on me like that?*

Not a single thought was evident on her face as she
kept the expression her grandfather had taught her to
wear whenever she played cards and nodded toward the
chair. "Knock yourself out."

Ian perched on the edge of the chair, looking as uncomfortable as someone sitting on red-hot coals.

Small talk was not something he indulged in, but for
now it seemed like a way of trying to smooth out the
rough waves between them. "I saw you on that award
show last week. Your grandfather still looks the way he
did when he was on *Savage Ben.*"

He didn't add that seeing her on the small screen had
brought a flood of feelings back, nearly drowning him
in them. That since he'd walked out of this studio, he
had been struggling every single day to keep his head
above water, to swim away from his feelings for her.
None of it had worked.

She nodded. They were talking like two strangers,
she thought. And maybe, despite the lovemaking, they
were. Because the man she'd thought she'd fallen in
love with never would have left her to mark time alone
in this living hell she found herself in.

"I'll tell him you said that." She forced herself to
focus on her grandfather. "It'll make him feel good."

"Good," he echoed, nodding.

Why was he here? Why had he come back? To torture her? To see if she was functioning without him? She drew herself up, determined to make him believe that she was doing just fine.

"Okay, I don't have time for this. I've got to go on in a few minutes, why are you here?"

He didn't answer directly. "I just got in an hour ago. I was on the West Coast."

Dakota pressed her lips together. Okay, since he didn't look any the worse for wear, she could pretend his being here in this small space wasn't driving her crazy. "Business?"

He stared down at his hands. Since when had his courage flagged like this? But then he realized that it took more courage to walk back into this dressing room than it did to chase an armed killer down a darkened alley. "Pleasure, actually."

Dakota fixed him with a stony look. "What does this have to do with me?"

Because it seemed as if everything in his life these days had something to do with her, he thought. "I was there because of you."

He was going to tell her about another woman. She rose to her feet, ready to usher him out before she said something she couldn't take back. Crossing to the door, she threw it open. "Glad to hear that I helped you learn to unwind, but—"

He made no move to rise to his feet, never took his eyes off her. "I went to see Scottie, the way you suggested." The surprised look on her face was priceless.

Dakota slowly closed the door again and retraced her steps to the dressing table, never taking her eyes off him. "Marla didn't look too happy to see me, but I made her understand that it was good for Scottie to have some kind of contact with me once in a while. To know that his father loved him and was thinking about him."

Words she'd said to him. So he had been listening after all. Dakota nodded. "I'm glad you did that," she said. More than words could express. She'd ached for Scottie when Ian had told her that his ex-wife had made it clear she didn't want him seeing the boy. Ached for Scottie and for him.

"Yeah, so am I. He's a really great kid," he said in a voice that fathers had been using to brag about their sons since the beginning of time. "We spent two weeks together. I even took him fishing. Him and Brian."

"Brian?"

"The man Marla married." It felt odd talking about his ex-wife's husband. Maybe he had come a long way in a short time, he thought. And if he had, it was all because of Dakota. "Brian's a pretty decent guy. He and Scottie like each other and get along."

Finding out that his son was well adjusted, that his son still loved him, had loosened a huge knot he'd been carrying around in his gut.

Restless, he rose again to stand over her. He slipped his hands into his back pockets, then pulled them out again, as if he didn't know what to do with them. With himself. And wouldn't until he finally said what he'd come to say.

Ian tried again. "Look, I botched up my first marriage."

"Usually takes two to botch."

He shrugged. "Maybe that's so, but I had the lion's share." A disparaging smile played along his lips as he looked at her. "You might have noticed that I don't communicate too well."

It took effort not to laugh. He had the gift of understatement, she'd give him that. "Yes, I noticed."

He felt like a man running to catch the last train out of the station before it departed and left him stranded. He'd been stranded far too long. He didn't want to be any longer. "But I can work on it."

A strange peacefulness began to descend over her. "Admirable goal. You do realize this requires that you give more than an occasional grunt in response."

"Yes, I realize that." He began to pace, then caught himself at it and stopped. "I also realize that I can't go back."

"To see Scottie?"

"No, to what there was before." His eyes searched hers, as if he was willing her to understand. "Because there wasn't anything before."

Far from understanding, Dakota felt as if she was sinking hip deep into a bog. Either she'd missed something, or he was getting things very, very garbled. She opted for the latter. "You still have a long way to go about learning how to use words to their best capacity."

Ian took a breath. It was all or nothing. "Okay, how's this? I don't like my life without you."

Now *that* she could understand. Dakota didn't even try to keep the wide smile from her lips. "I'd say you just went to the head of the remedial speech class with a very good chance of acing the final."

He took her hands in his, drawing her to him. "My life feels hollow without you."

There was her heart, taking that all-too-familiar trip up to her throat again. Breathing was becoming a challenge. "Excellent."

"And I love you." There, they were out, the fatal words that bound him to her.

This time it took her almost a full minute to drag air back into her lungs. Her heart beat wildly. "Very good," she whispered, her voice almost cracking from the weight of emotion.

"Will you stop grading me, Dakota, and tell me I'm not making a fool of myself?"

She could only parrot what he said. "You're not making a fool of yourself."

A warmth began to spread through his limbs. He'd made it, made it out of his lonely hovel of an existence, and crossed the chasm to hers. "And that you feel something, too."

She couldn't focus, couldn't think, could only feel. And it was wonderful. "And I feel something, too."

"Dakota—"

Humor danced in her blue eyes. She could have sworn that she was having an out-of-body experience. The only extraneous thing she felt was the cameo. It felt as if it was glowing against her flesh. "A whole lot of somethings," she told him.

He shook his head, rejecting the paltry offering. "Too nebulous. Words, woman, give me words. You're the one who knows how to use them."

She laughed. "And yet, suddenly, I'm tongue-tied."

"Look, I know this is a lot to spring on you all of a sudden like this, but—"

If he was going to take it back, she didn't want to hear it. Dakota placed her finger against his lips. Stopped midword, he looked at her in surprise.

"No, it's not. I'm just surprised, that's all. It's been a whole month, Ian. You didn't call, you didn't write, there wasn't even a carrier pigeon on my windowsill. Thirty-two days, nothing."

He knew exactly how long it had been down to the second. "I was trying to get over you."

She cupped his cheek with her palm. "I'm not the flu, Ian. You don't have to 'get over' me." And she prayed that once "infected" he never would. "People spend their whole lives looking for love. I know, I'm one of them."

Ian waited for her to say more. When she didn't, he prodded. "And?"

"And what?"

"Do you think you found it?"

A smile feathered along her lips. "I might need some persuading."

"I'll see what I can do." Taking her into his arms, Ian kissed her. Long and hard and with all the feeling that an entire month's worth of abstinence could generate. Until that very moment, he hadn't realized just how much he'd missed her. And how much he never wanted them to be separated again. The loneliness he had lived with for the last month disappeared in the heat of their contact.

Finally drawing back, he looked down into her face. "How's that?"

"Very good," she whispered, then cleared her throat to try to regain some kind of control over at least her voice. Her body, she acknowledged, was pretty much a lost cause. "For an opening argument," she qualified mischievously.

For the first time since he'd walked into her dressing room, Ian grinned at her. Maybe this was going to work out after all. "I've got a hell of a closer."

She tried not to laugh. Delight felt as if it was shining out of every pore. "I just bet you do."

Unable to help himself, Ian kissed her again. As the kiss grew, weakening them both, he knew that at any moment, he was in danger of giving in to his desire to make love with her. But as much as he wanted to, the minutes were ticking away and she was due on the set. So he held himself in check as best he could.

And pushed his argument forward.

"I've decided to take an executive advisory position at the firm."

Her head was still spinning. Why was he talking about work at a time like this? "What does that mean?"

"It means the only body I'll be guarding on a regular basis is yours."

He'd already talked it out with Randy. There was no way he was going to take assignments that would keep him away from her, night and day. That was for people who didn't have a reason to come home at night. He had a feeling that he was going to have a reason, a very good reason, very soon.

"I want to marry you, Dakota." Her mouth fell open. Very gently, with the tip of his finger, Ian pushed it closed again. "You don't have to answer right away," he cautioned, afraid that she would turn him down. "Think about it."

"How long do I have to think about it?"

He couldn't read her expression. Nerves surfaced. "As long as you want."

"Oh. Okay." She pressed her lips together, then whispered, "Yes."

He couldn't believe his ears. Or his luck.

"Damn it, Dakota, I can't hear you." MacKenzie's voice came barging in through the door. "You'd better have said yes."

She laughed softly, shaking her head as she looked toward the door.

"I said yes." And then she looked back at Ian. She was relieved that he didn't look annoyed or upset by her friend's intrusion. "We have an audience."

He took it in stride. All that mattered was that she'd said yes. "I figure, you being who you are, we always will." His arms tightened around her. "But that doesn't mean we can't create our own world away from them if you're willing."

He loved her, she thought, and he wanted to marry her. Everything else could be worked out.

"*So* willing you have no idea." And then, suddenly, surprising him, she swatted at his shoulder. "I could kill you for putting me through this."

Nothing was going to spoil his mood. "You have the rest of our lives to make me pay."

"Don't think I won't."

He grinned. "I'm looking forward to it." He pressed a kiss to her temple. "I can't wait for Scottie to meet you."

The full import of his words, of what was happening, hit her. She could hardly believe it. "Wow, a husband and a son, all in one big swoop."

Concern surfaced. Was he going too fast for her after all? "Too much?"

It was perfect, all perfect. She framed his face in her hands. "Just the beginning. I love kids." Rising on her toes, she teased his lips with hers. "And I love you most of all."

For the first time in his life, he felt truly at peace. As if from here on in, everything was ultimately going to be all right. He was too much of a realist not to believe that there wouldn't be storms along the way, but together they could weather anything. "I'm going to need proof."

"After the show!" MacKenzie's voice came through the door again. There was a pleading note in it.

But it fell on deaf ears.

Epilogue

September 1, 1863

Amanda abandoned the dress she was attempting to make over for her younger sister. It had been hers once, but she no longer cared about dressing up in finery. With Will on the battlefield, the reason for music had gone out of her life.

Susannah was still young and needed to feel that there was a future, where dances would be held and young men would return to whisper in her ear—young men who now faced the risk of being devoured by a war whose tide had turned against them.

In the distance she saw her father riding toward the house. Alexander Deveaux was on horseback now, where once he would have taken a carriage. But the carriage was as broken as his spirit was, its carcass left to rot in the field because there was no clever hand to fix it. Her older brother, Jonathan, had fallen at Chancellorville, and the light had gone out of her father's eyes.

Dismounting, Alexander handed the reins to Old Jacob. The latter had elected to remain even though he was now emancipated and free to make his way wherever he chose. Old Jacob told anyone who would listen that he had chosen here.

Her father strode toward the front porch. "Amanda, there's news."

Amanda jumped to her feet. Her heart slammed against her chest. "A letter? Is there a letter from Will?"

She searched her father's face, praying that the solemn expression she saw there was just his concern about the state of the economy and their swiftly dwindling fortune. That it had nothing to do with her fiancé.

Her hand closed around the cameo she never took off.

Will had been away for nearly three years now. Three years that were broken up only by the arrival of much-stained, much-creased letters. They had been few and far between, many, she suspected, having been lost in their journey from his hand to hers.

The tone of the letters over the last year had worried her. Hope seemed to have left Will's soul. But there had been no letters these past few months. Not a single missive, nothing to set her fearful heart at ease. She had no idea where he was, if he was cold or hungry or even—please God, no—wounded.

She would not allow herself to think anything worse. It was hard enough grieving for her brother.

"There are lists," her father said. He slipped his arm around her shoulders to ease the burden of what he knew they were about to bear. "Lists of our wounded," Alexander began.

Her heart froze within her breast. "Is his name on there?" she cried. "Does it say Will's wounded?"

If he were wounded, would he be coming home to mend? Tyler Banks had been wounded in the very first battle, and he had come back to his wife and children. Wherever Will was, she made up her mind to go to him, to be with him and tend to his wounds until he was well again. Mama wouldn't want her to go, but that didn't matter. She'd go anywhere in the world, so long as Will needed her.

"And of the missing," her father continued stoically. He looked down at her. "William Slattery's name is on that list."

A strange pulsing began in her ears. "Will?" she repeated in disbelief. It couldn't be true. He was too alive, too full of life to be missing.

Her father nodded, his hand tightening on her shoulder. "They could not find him after the battle of Gettysburg."

Amanda's heart sank like a stone. The world around

her shrank away from her until there was nothing left but a pinprick of light.

And then that was gone, too.

* * * * *

If you liked BECAUSE A HUSBAND IS FOREVER,
you'll love Marie Ferrarella's next romance,
A BABY CHANGES EVERYTHING,
part of Signature's continuity,
THE FORTUNES OF TEXAS: REUNION.
Coming to you July 2005.
Don't miss it!

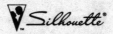

SPECIAL EDITION™

Don't miss the exciting conclusion of
The Fortunes of Texas: Reunion
three-book continuity
in Silhouette Special Edition

IN A TEXAS MINUTE
by Stella Bagwell

Available April 2005
Silhouette Special Edition #1677

When Sierra Mendoza was left with an abandoned
baby, she turned to her closest friend and confidant,
Alex Calloway. While taking care of the infant,
Sierra and Alex's relationship went from platonic
to passionate. But would deep-seated scars from Alex's
past prevent them from becoming a ready-made family?

THE
FORTUNES
OF TEXAS:
Reunion

The price of privilege. The power of family.

Available at your favorite retail outlet.

Where love comes alive™

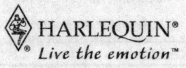